Amy Redek

Farell

Hot Romance Erotica

WARNING

This book contains sexually explicit scenes and adult language. It may be considered offensive to some readers. This book is for sale to adults ONLY.

* * * * * * * * * * * * * * * * * *

Please store your files wisely where they cannot be accessed by underage readers.

Please feel free to send me an email. Just know that these emails are filtered by my publisher. Good news is always welcome.

Amy Redek - **amy_redek@awesomeauthors.org**

You might also want to check my blog for Updates and interesting info.
http://amy-redek.awesomeauthors.org/

About the Publisher

4Fun Publishing, a member of **BLVNP Incorporated**, 340 S. Lemon #6200, Walnut CA 91789, info@blvnp.com / legal@blvnp.com
NOTE: Due to the highly emotional reaction of some people to works of erotic fiction, any email sent to the above address that contains foul language or religious references is automatically deleted by our anti-spam software and will not be seen. All other communications are welcome.

DISCLAIMER

Please don't be stupid and kill yourself. This book is a work of FICTION. Do not try any new sexual practice that you find in this book. It is fiction and not to be confused with reality. Neither the author nor the publisher or its associates assume any responsibility for any loss, injury, death or legal consequences resulting from acting on the contents in this book. Every character in this book is over 18 years of age. The author's opinions are not to be construed as the opinions of the publisher. The material in this book is for entertainment purposes ONLY. Enjoy.

FARELL

Hot Romance Erotica

By: Amy Redek

Chapter One

'It was a dark and stormy night and the lightening crashed and the thunder flashed,' I began before being interrupted by a bright seven-year-old girl.

'Excuse me, Mr. Farrell,' her right arm held up high, 'but shouldn't that be the lightning flashed and the thunder crashed?'

'Quite right, my young Miss. I changed the words to see if you were paying attention,' which proved that at least one was. This was becoming my party piece as I was always invited to the birthday parties of my niece and nephew and as the end of the party was nigh, I would always be asked to tell a ghost story. The floor would be cleared and we would only have the light of a solitary candle on the mantel piece behind me as the children sat in a semi-circle before me, holding hands. So in the gloom of the room with just this single flickering light that didn't show my features, I had to make the most of the story with the tones of my voice. They liked it when it was deep and sonorous to try and portray that somewhere outside of our circle was a mysterious and threatening presence. One year I didn't begin with those words and I had cries of dismay, so ever since, I've had to begin my stories the same way. They understood these words whether it be around an old house alone in the middle of the moors, or a castle perched high on a cliff edge with the seas crashing and rolling against the sharp jagged rocks that had seen many ships founder. They could imagine the single flashing light high up in the castle, luring a ship to its destruction on the rocks below.

These were pictures they could conjure up in their mind's eye as I described the wind and the way that it talks to man, bird and beast. This was the beginning to their story and it was not to be left out though the critics say that a book should never open with these lines, but it was the way that my critics who sat before me all wanted it to begin.

But my own story for you really started with it being quite the opposite, though if I ever got to tell it to the children, it would have to be different. Spring had arrived and the sun was shining and all seemed right with the world. My name is Michael Farrell and I'm slightly overweight for my height of six foot if taken with my being thirty two years of age. I have light blue eyes, clean shaven, average features and have brown to black coloured hair which is of no value to the story but just helps to fill up the picture for you to see me.

I live alone in a cottage, of which there are twelve in what is known as Meadows Lane that leads nowhere from the lane at the top. This top lane, or road is one of those nightmare thoroughfares that only has passing areas about two hundred yards apart. Not lay-bys but just bits of ground where the hedge has been crushed over the years and were now just bare patches of earth that were full of mud and icy water during the winter. Many's the time you can hear the honking of horns as two vehicles meet and neither want to reverse to clear the way. It is usually the one with a female inside that finally gives way and makes the tricky job of reversing round a blind bend to be able to pull into the hedge lined gap.

This was the road at the top of my lane and it had just a small pub and one shop that sold a lot of nothing, and to complete this part of the village, there were six cottages either side of these two public places. These were all on the right as we came out and turned left from Meadows Lane because the land opposite and onto which my cottage backed, was Meadows Farm.

It was over a quarter of a mile before we came to the stables on the right and this was directly opposite another lane that ran in the same direction as the one I lived in. Now this would show the ingenuity of the district's planning many years ago, because it bounded the other side of Meadows Farm and that my lane was called Meadows Lane, they named this one by just dropping the letter S. Brilliant thinking on someone's part. This lane too had twelve cottages and so it was almost a mirror image to mine if one could look down from above.

Now at the bottom of the two lanes and of the farm in between, was what were locally known as the cliffs. A misnomer if ever there was one like calling our hamlet a village. Our cliffs were about twenty foot high and as the land and soil slowly broke away with wind and rain, they became slopes that ran down to a narrow pebbled beach, if I could even call it that. Though the land of the farm was flat where the farmhouse stood, it rose up towards the sea end but rolled down on either side to where the lanes were, so from where I lived, I couldn't see the lane on the other side of these fields because of this small hill.

I know, I know, you're getting impatient for me to start the story but I had to give you the lay out and topography of the place first and you'll understand why in a minute. Now I'll get to the problem I caused our postie, postman to you townies, his name by the way is Pat. Well, that is what everybody calls him like they call our village Toy Town. We don't have a Noddy but we do have a Big Ears, but due to the size of the fellow, no one has ever dared call him that. Built like a brick..., er, outhouse, with arms and shoulders that many a tree would be proud to have limbs like that. He was much in demand at harvest time because he could pitch fork even the most soggiest of hay bales to toss it over twenty feet high onto the hay wagon.

But the problem I caused our postman was of my surname Farrell, because there was another man of that name in the opposite lane, only his Christian name was Nicholas. When we did eventually meet, it became Mick and Nick, mine coming first alphabetically. What compounded postman Pat's problem was none of the cottages had numbers or names and he delivered by the surname on the letter, so sometimes I got Nick's and he got mine if the writer dropped the letter S. Also I think Pat had an eye problem to tell the difference between the two letters of our Christian names.

It was a joke when it first happened as I got a letter that was meant for Nick and so I took a walk along the cliffs and over the hill to hand deliver it myself for which he opened a bottle of beer as a thank you. Then another day he delivered one to me and I reciprocated with a bottle of beer and a chat. Now this would happen three, maybe four times a year so we both now always kept a few bottles of beer available in the pantry as payment.

It was on this glorious spring morning that Pat delivered one for Nick to my cottage, so after I had my breakfast and washed up and put the things away decided to take over his letter. I put it in my jacket pocket and went out into the garden but stopped as I looked at the sorry state of my roses. I saw that they could do with a bit of nutrient about now if I wanted a good showing this year, so decided to call in at the stables first to order some manure.

I walked up my lane and turned left and gave a wave to Dave, the pub landlord as he was seeing to his weekly delivery by the draymen. I ambled along the lane, keeping one ear cocked for the sound of any approaching vehicle from either direction, but as we are such a way off the beaten track, we don't get that many. I called in at the stables and spoke to the head lad; lad? He was nearly double my age and agreed to drop a couple of bags off at my cottage though I stressed that only when there was time and not to rush, which was a bit of a joke because nobody rushed in Toy Town.

With the manure ordered, I then went down the lane to Nick's cottage and I called out as I entered the garden but only got silence as a response. I went round to his back door which was never locked and went in, calling out his name again. The kitchen was clean and tidy but still no Nick. I went and felt the tea cloth and found that it was damp which told me he'd eaten and washed up. I went to his pantry and took out a bottle of beer and put it in the middle of the table so that it was a reminder of what he owed me as I propped his letter up against it.

I went out closing the door and down through his garden for the walk along the cliffs back to my place. It certainly was a pleasure to walk through the grass and feel the first hint of warmth from the sun on my back so I took my jacket off and slung it over my shoulder, enjoying the slight breeze coming off the sea and I could hear what I thought were larks as I got near the top of the small hill.

It was by looking up into the sky and not looking where I was putting my feet that I tripped and went sprawling flat down on my stomach, and as I raised my head, came face to face with Nick. There, in the grass, eyes half closed and the mouth fixed in a rictus of a grin, a foot away from me was Nick's head.

Chapter Two

I've seen many dead people in my life, but it was the sudden shock of seeing his head there that made me suddenly roll over several times to rise up on my knees and vomit. I wiped my mouth after spitting a few times, with my handkerchief, and now looked and saw that it was his body that I had tripped over. My first thought was, why Nick? Then came the how? How many people walk about the English countryside carrying a machete or sword slung at their waist? Oh you poor bastard, I thought as I looked at his head so far from his body but knew better than to bring the two together. With not a soul in sight there wasn't anything I could do except get to my cottage and phone for the police, so at a stumbling run, I made for home.

'Police?' I asked when I got through. 'I wish to report a murder at the far end of Meadows Farm.'

'How do you know it's murder, sir?' was the polite query from the other end.

'With the head six feet away from the body, I ruled out suicide,' I said sarcastically. Giving them my name and address, I was told to stay there and a car would be dispatched immediately. It still took them nearly thirty minutes to come down the lane and with them looking quizzically at all twelve cottages, went out and made myself known to them.

'You found the body, sir?' the sergeant asked me. 'Where is it?' I said yes to the first question and took them through my garden up the cliff walk and over the rise to where Nick's body lay. When it came into view, he told me and the other two policemen to stop and he went on by himself. He didn't go too close before coming back and instructing one of them to stay there to see that nobody else went near it.

As we walked back to my cottage, he was speaking into his mobile walkie talkie attached to the shoulder of his uniform asking for a forensic team, giving them brief details plus directions. By the time he had finished we were at the cottage and we went inside and they accepted a cup of tea as I related my movements of the morning while the policeman wrote in his notebook. As we finished, another car drew up outside with a van pulling up behind it.

'Constable,' the sergeant said. 'Go with the forensic team and take them through the farm to where the body is.' As he went out, two obviously plain clothes policemen came in.

'My name is Detective Inspector Loomis and this is Detective Constable Dawkins, Mr.....?' he asked with his hand extended which I shook as the Sergeant tended my name.

'Farrell, sir.'

'Mr. Farrell. I understand you found the body?'

'Yes. Nicholas Farrell of Meadow Lane.'

'Farrell? A relative?'

'No. Just one of those quirks of fate that we are, were, both in the village at the same time with the same name.'

'Yes, quite. That will be all sergeant, we'll take over from here. Collect your men and thank you for being so prompt.'

Exit stage right the sergeant and constable.

'May we sit down, Mr. Farrell?'

'I'm sorry, of course. Would you like tea or something?'

'No, thank you,' he said as they sat down. 'Now tell me what you know of the other Mr. Farrell, your connection with him and what happened today?' So I related as much as I could of Nick and of how I found his body.

'What did you have for breakfast this morning, sir?' D.C. Dawkins asked of me, 'and what you also had for dinner last night?' I knew why he asked so I told him and felt sorry for the person who would have to analyse what I'd left up on the hill to prove my statement.

'May I ask what your occupation is, Mr. Farrell?'

'You may, but I'm afraid you'll have to make that enquiry of room forty two at the Foreign Office for an answer,' I replied.

'Oh, I see,' he said slowly. 'Well, let's go and visit the scene of the crime.' So D.I. Loomis, D.C. Dawkins and myself left the cottage and went up the small hill to where the forensic people had set up some screens. I was now able to view Nick's body dispassionately as the others did and let my thoughts wander as to the why. I had my thoughts as to the who because it had all the hallmarks of an Arabic execution, but which faction I couldn't say at this time. There were quite a few I had upset over the last few years, but how had they got my name? How did they know where to find me? The answer was to go to London to find out.

Chapter Three

When I got to my usual reporting station, I found a message for me to go and see Jackson, head of my department. Well, not just mine as he was really the head honcho of the whole shebang and had been working for him for the past four years.

'Farrell?' He exclaimed as I entered at his call after knocking at his door. 'That was damned quick. I only sent a car an hour ago for you, what did you do, fly back?'

'No, sir. Something happened yesterday that I think is serious enough for me to come and see you for I think I've been compromised,' and went on to tell him what happened in Toy Town and the conclusions that I had arrived at. The thing I liked about Jackson was the fact that whatever you had to say, he listened without making any interruptions, making notes till you had finished before speaking himself.

'It seems they are slightly ahead of us. It's what I feared and why I dispatched the car for you. You are correct in the fact that you have been compromised and I have pity for that other man, but it's a question of there, but for the grace of God. Him having the same name as you is what saved you from his fate.

'We've worked out that it was a splinter group of the Ba'athists that ordered your execution in reprisal for what you did the last time you were out there. Matheson's body was dumped outside our Embassy only six hours ago. The doctor who examined his wounds believed he lasted eight hours under their torture and it has now been proved that they got quite a bit of information out of him before he died. The saving grace was that they didn't have a picture of you and so believe they have succeeded in their mission.'

'Have they been identified yet?'

'I believe so, but it has yet to be confirmed. The suspects are now in Dublin and,' he looked at his watch, 'about to board the flight for Paris. There's a helicopter on the pad waiting to take you to the airport where a private jet is ready to take you to Paris. Lewis, you know Lewis?'

'Yes,' my thoughts racing at this sudden turn of events.

'But of course you know him. He'll give you more details on landing because we believe they'll be catching a plane there for Teheran and you are to follow them, but do not stop them. Let them report a successful mission and we can deal with them later.'

'I still don't know who they are?' I protested.

'We'll both know for sure by the time you get to Paris. Good luck, Michael. Oh, that we'll have to change when you get back.'

So that would be the end of Toy Town for me, I thought as I was escorted upstairs to the helicopter pad on the roof of the building. Four years of a home now gone plus what could have been a long lasting friendship, something I'd not had so far in my life. The pilot of the helicopter saw that my straps were fixed properly before he lifted off to take me to Heathrow where we landed ten minutes later. An airport car was waiting which quickly took me to a small jet that already had its turbines turning over waiting, and was beginning to move before the door had closed properly.

It was taxiing as the door was closed and I was shown where to sit and had only just buckled up my seat belt before it was taking off with immediate clearance from the tower. So much for travelling on government business. I still didn't know what I was supposed to be doing but Jackson had just over the hour to get that sorted out for Lewis to instruct me when we got to Paris.

***

'Hello, Mike,' he greeted me as I stepped off the jet at a place out of sight of the terminal. 'Let's talk in the car,' so I followed him and got into an airport car, without driver, to talk. 'I'm glad they missed you, Mike,' Lewis said.

'So am I but my friend isn't,' I said sourly, 'but it won't be Mike anymore, will it?'

'No, and I'm sorry for your friend, but, well, what about poor Matheson?' He gave a cough and opened one of these flat kind of carrying cases and drew out a wad of paper and documents. 'New passport in the name of Phillip Travers, oil pipe line construction surveyor. All verified with the oil company in London that you've been working for them for the past ten years. Brief history here,' as he handed me three close typed sheets of paper. 'The photographs and names of the two assassins for you to study but not touch. Jackson was most emphatic on this. Leave them alone for they will be dealt with later now that we know them. Your job is to follow them where ever they go and more importantly, find where their headquarters are. We believe it is the region of the geological maps in this case that you are going to survey for a possible pipe line, along with all the necessary permits for you to travel about the area. Also there are five thousand pounds of the local currency and ten thousand U.S. dollars and Jackson has asked for you to bring back the change please.

'We are staying in the Teheran Hilton for our first night and play it by ear from then on. If you've finished with the brief and the photos, I'll have them back.' I had been reading them as he had been speaking and having got the basic gist of them along with knowing that I would recognise my two friends again, passed them back to him. He put them into another small case which I recognised as a mini incinerator and that any paper or inflammable material placed inside and the catch operated properly, burnt to a crisp whatever was put inside in a matter of seconds without smoke or fumes.

'Now let's get to the terminal and mingle before the flight,' he said as he gave a signal to a waiting man who got into the driving seat and drove us to where we could slip in unobserved. Lewis had already prepared a grip for me with clothing that befitted my new persona, so with ticket, passport and grip, I presented myself at the airline check-in and was passed through into the departure area to await the calling of my flight.

I casually strolled through the shops seeking the two men but it wasn't till after the flight was called and in that small holding lounge did I spot them. I also noticed that Lewis had picked them up too. What pissed me off was that I then saw, as the boarding began, that Lewis had a first class ticket while I had to sit and suffer in economy class. Thankfully it was a French airline so I was able to have with my meal a vodka and tonic, my last drop of alcohol until I got out of Iran.

It was bloody hot when we landed and was thankful to get to the hotel and into the air conditioning. I forgot how hot it could get out there and hoped that Lewis had remembered to pack some sun blocking cream in with my kit. Lewis hadn't come with me to the hotel because he had been picked up by a waiting car that followed our two men to find out where they would be spending the night. He also had some local ground operatives standing by to watch them and report their movements within the city.

The first thing I did on checking in was to ask the front desk for them to hire me a four-wheel drive vehicle and an English speaking driver, letting them see my oil papers and permits. I mangled what appeared to be the only Arabic words I knew in this request concealing the fact that I spoke the language fluently. I knew I was going to be grossly overcharged and wasn't disappointed when I was told how much a day it would cost me. I shrugged and had to accept the figure they gave me, listening to their spoken asides as they silently laughed at me for being another stupid business man.

I later met up with Lewis in the bar and only accepted a soft drink as we talked as two Englishmen would meeting up that far from home. With the barman finally getting called away from our end of the bar where we sat, he brought me up to date with where they were and that they were expected to leave Teheran the following morning by bus. Before we parted, he passed across a small package that contained a magnetic tracking device and the responder which was about the size of and really did look like a mobile phone.

The driver of my Land Rover the next morning spoke English and was quite happy to go out shopping with me for supplies of food and camping equipment. He would haggle with the shopkeepers, taking nearly twenty five per cent as a back hander with every purchase we made, chalking up about seven hundred pounds for which he would suffer later.

With all that I needed, we returned to the hotel where I still had time for a shower and to change into decent travelling clothes for the desert before I had to relinquish the room. I met Lewis in the bar and he told me what bus our targets had boarded, passing across the route of it saying that they probably wouldn't disembark until near the end of its scheduled run. Then I had to somehow get the tracking device onto any vehicle that might pick them up.

The bus had a two-hour start on us but I didn't push my driver knowing that we would be up to the bus by about midafternoon. I gave him the direction and off we set in pursuit of the bus and after four hours driving, I had him stop at the next village for a break and some tea. Nearly a pound for a small glass was exorbitant, but I didn't argue but paid what was asked and got a couple of sweetmeats thrown in free. Now I made the excuse to sit in the back so that I could spread my maps to study the terrain as we travelled, also to check the stopping points of the bus so that I could have him pull off the road for me to observe who got off.

We passed the bus just after three o'clock and now it was time for me to start having the driver zigzagging across the sands so that we were never far from the bus and I could get to a vantage point to see who left it when it stopped. It was about an hour before nightfall and it almost caught me unawares when the bus stopped it appeared, to be in the middle of nowhere. It was only by using my telescopic sight could I then discern a track and my two would-be executioners get off and let the bus go on its way.

I made a quick study of the terrain and got back into our car and told the driver to get back down to the road and had him head in the same direction of the bus. I could see the two men in the distance waiting, and at the same time, a land rover coming out of the desert to obviously meet them. We were still a mile or two away when the jeep came up to the two men and after a few minutes they climbed aboard and the jeep reversed its course and set off again.

My driver couldn't understand when I ordered him to turn off the road onto the track to follow the jeep. Our speed was faster and it was soon in sight and I urged him on faster to catch it up and get them to stop. He began flashing his lights and sounding his horn as we got closer and the jeep eventually slowed and came to a stop and we pulled up just behind them.

'Ask them how far it is to the next village,' I instructed my driver. So we both got out for him to ask the question while I did some stretching exercises and then went round kicking our tyres and eventually moved over to the jeep and asked him what the answer was. While doing this, I placed the transmitter just under the spare wheel on the rear door of their jeep before he turned to give me the answer.

'Too far along this track before nightfall. They suggest we either go back to the road or sleep out here because it will be dark soon,' he reported back. It was close enough to what they had said between them in Arabic so I agreed that we would tent out for the night. My driver thanked and bid them farewell and as they drove off, began to get our gear out for setting up camp for the night. I went back to my maps showing no interest in the departing jeep as he began to erect my tent.

Having seen where the men had got off the bus and knowing exactly how far we had come down this track, I knew precisely where we were. I watched anxiously my tracking device getting more unsettled the further and further it was moving away from me. Then to my relief, it stopped moving at just under one hundred and twenty miles away and by turning the device one way and then another, was able to near enough pin point on my map where they had stopped.

Thankfully I turned it off and had the meal that my driver had prepared for me before turning in for the night. I was up before first light and going away a little for a pee and a crap, tuned into the tracking signal and was pleased that it was still stationary. I spent the whole of that day making the appearance of surveying the area and studying the terrain, but keeping an eye on my transponder. The signal didn't move, and nor had it moved the next morning so I told the driver I'd seen enough and to get us back to the city.

The driver was happy enough to go back after sleeping two nights in the car and now he would soon get paid. I made him wait outside the hotel while I checked in and had a word with Lewis, telling him to have his friends ready near the garage where the car came from. I then got my gear from the car and paid the driver and thirty minutes later he was stopped, robbed and all the camping equipment stolen. This paid off all of Lewis's hired hands and after a bath and a good night's sleep in a bed instead of on sand, flew out of Teheran the following morning.

For two days, experts studied the satellite photographs of my location of this terrorist camp and confirmed its existence but had no signs of life at each pass of this surveillance equipment. But we knew that they knew the times when this spy in the sky was due to pass over and so all activity ceased until it had passed. It spite of this enormous amount of inactivity, two stealth bombers flew into Iranian air space at low level and blew the place apart and were back out inside of twelve minutes.

Chapter Four

I was shown the satellite photographs taken after the air attack in Jackson's office and there wasn't a sign left of the encampment and the Iranian government was screaming blue murder about a violation of their air space but made no mention of a bombing attack on a terrorist camp.

'That was a good job you did, Phillip,' Jackson said. So I was now to be Phillip Travers of no fixed abode in his eyes, well to hell with him. My name was Michael Farrell and as I was now presumed to be dead by these terrorists, I couldn't see any reason for my not returning to Toy Town. He raised an eyebrow when I told him where I was going but saw the logic to it and didn't demure. But before I went home I decided to drop in on Lewis not having seen him at the office. The office is what we called the section where Jackson sat like a spider in the middle of his web, listening and feeling all the vibrations throughout the world. Just picture in your mind how a spider's web looks like when you've come across one in the garden of a field or wood. From the centre there are many threads that move out to the final ring and in between these are many circles joining the whole together.

The first inner circle would be the international desks and the thread running out being their line of communication, now for where every ring touches this thread is another desk and so on. The rings themselves are either operatives or informers or gatherers of information that feed it round to the desk nearest them.

So if there is the slightest tremor in one of the circles of this web, its vibration is fed to the thread that leads to the centre. Small tremors may only reach the first desk, but high powered ones then get fed up the line and if it is deemed worthy of action may even reach the centre where Jackson sat. I was just part of one thread but being out on one of the rings as it were though I must say I was on a ring that was very close to the centre.

Lewis was my field officer where I was known as a field operative. Not 007, licensed to kill and all that, but I could get away with it if it was in the national interest, or more bluntly, my own survival in a sticky situation. It was his job to set things up like this last one, that is getting me papers, supplying me with a false identity and background, money and being a backup. I've somewhat over simplified his job but that is the basics of what he does, though it would take far too long to really go into in depth. There were too many inconsistencies in this affair that was nagging me and before I wanted to start to draw conclusions, I had to know a bit more of what Lewis knew or had been told.

There's always this need to know basis, which is a good thing for if caught, you cannot, even under torture, divulge what you don't know. You might make up stories to try and end the torture which would mean your death, or make something up to either prolong the torture in the hope that you would be rescued, which in itself is fanciful. It was more to hope that you might, just might be able to escape in the interim period of them checking out what you have told them.

But being the curious bugger that I am, I always needed to know more than I should, like I knew where Lewis lived and where he went for a drink and so on. I made it a point to know as much about him as he knew about me which was a damn sight more.

So after swanning about London for a while, I finally made my way to Chelsea to a pub where I knew that Lewis went for a drink. Boy, did he jump when I tapped him on the shoulder and asked for a vodka and tonic.

'What the bloody hell are you doing here?' were his first startled words.

'Asking for you to get me a drink,' I said mildly.

'With ice?' he asked sarcastically.

'Naturellemont,' I replied sitting down, pleased at his discomfiture at being found by me of all people. He got up and got himself another beer and my drink and returned to the table.

'What the hell are you doing here?' he asked again.

'Need to know basis, Lewis, a need to know,' I said as I put my hand on his and squeezed it hard. 'I need to know who set me up?' I said fiercely in a low harsh voice.

'Matheson broke,' he said, having to use force to get my hand off his.

'Bollocks. They knew where I lived whereas Matheson didn't and that's just for starters.'

'What do you mean?' he asked, rubbing his wrist.

'Okay, I'll come back to that in a minute,' I said somewhat wearily. 'When were you told to set up this operation we've just finished?'

'About four hours before you arrived in Paris. I was there at the embassy and got woken up and told to cobble it together. I thought I did a bloody good job in the time frame.'

'And this was the first you knew of it? When you were woken up, I mean?'

'Yes, why?'

'I'm just trying to put the pieces of this jigsaw together because some of the pieces don't fit.'

'In what way?'

'Okay, I'll try and make it as simple as I can. Jackson sends a car for me at eight in the morning because he's found out that Matheson has been tortured and killed, dumped outside our embassy, but of which one? This hasn't been said. Jackson didn't mention where he was found and it took him around four hours before sending a car for me. What was the link between me and Matheson?

'Next point is that if he was killed after torture, which according to the doctor must have lasted about eight hours judging by the state of his wounds, what time was he first taken? The doctor hadn't given a time of death or at least I wasn't told when he died, just the fact that he was dumped around four a.m. Now I don't see them keeping a body for very long before getting rid of it when they've got the information they want. But why advertise the fact? Why not just bury him? I believe Matheson was a red herring!'

'Oh come on,' Lewis protested. 'He got caught, tortured and killed and then they came after you.'

'No. That's where you are wrong. As I said at the beginning, Matheson didn't know where I lived plus the time frame's all wrong. They, the killers, were already in a remote part of Cornwall knowing where I was nearly twenty four hours before Matheson got taken. Matheson didn't tell them, they already knew!'

'Oh Christ,' Lewis breathed, the time element now sinking into his brain.

'As I said, I was a target and that they used Matheson to try and cover up that somebody else had given them my whereabouts.'

'Yes, yes, I see it now,' Lewis said. 'You don't think, no, it can't have been Jackson!'

'No. I'm certain it wasn't him and it was why I asked you when you were informed.'

'You didn't think it was me?' he looked and sounded shocked.

'Not really or I wouldn't be talking to you now.' I saw him give a little shudder though he tried to hide it for he knew I was a killer and that what I had said was true.

'Now I mean to find who set me up and you've got to help me, because I may not be the only one in the department who is being fingered to the opposition.'

Then came an incident that I'm not sure confirmed or didn't, my hypothesis of what was going on. I'd got another round of drinks in and then went to the toilet. I just finished having a pee and was washing my hands when the door opened and in walked Telford. Now this man was a known purveyor of lies, truths and half-truths. He lived by listening to other people's conversations and gleaning what he could and then selling what he learned to a willing recipient of either gossip or secrets.

His face went white when he saw me which was enough to make my hackles rise.

'Farrell! You're supposed to be dead!' was what he said and then he became so. It was the fact that the death of Nicholas Farrell had not been made public that prompted me to such quick action because he, of all people, shouldn't have known of my death. I would like to have got him to our basement to find out what he knew, but I'm afraid I was rather over exuberant in this case. As he uttered those words, my hand went up and with the hard edge, smashed it into his larynx and he went down like a pole axed bull. I couldn't take the chance and then twisted his head till I heard, and felt his neck snap.

I cursed myself as I went out of the toilets after heaving his body up off the floor and into a cubicle and pulled the door shut. I should have hit only to maim so as to get more out of him but it was the shock of him knowing the fact that I should be dead and didn't believe that he had connections to the Middle East that made me want to stop him from telling the world that I was still alive.

I went back to the table and quickly gulped down my drink.

'Drink up or leave it because we're leaving, now!' I said to Lewis.

'Why?' he asked with the pint glass halfway up to his mouth as he took a mouthful, then nearly lost it when I answered him.

'I've just killed Telford in the toilet.' It took some effort on his part not to splutter his beer all over the table, but managed to swallow what he had in his mouth. To give him his due, the glass went straight down onto the table and he got up and we left the bar and he got onto control with his mobile phone. When the connection was made, he asked for a clean-up squad, giving them the name of the pub and where the body was.

Somewhere deep in the bowels of our office building is a large underground garage where a variety of vehicles are stationed. Mostly vans with different logos painted on the sides as well as cars. There is always a squad of men on standby in case of emergencies and have various uniforms, overalls or other types of clothing to suit whatever purpose the leader decides on.

To collect a body that could cause a problem for the department was usually done very quietly, like from an hotel room or a private flat or house. It was more difficult when it was such a public place like a pub. The leader of the squad, Trevor Dasher, a very apt name for the speed he had to sometimes generate before the body was found, immediately called out to the men that they would be a bomb squad. So while they quickly found the appropriate clothing, he phoned the police for a cordon on the area while his second in command let the garage people downstairs know what vehicles they would need.

Such was their experience and control, they were there at the pub in just a shade over fourteen minutes, arriving just after the police. The street was quickly sealed off and people being asked to move back as the pub was entered and all told to leave immediately because of this report of a suspected bomb on the premises.

The bomb squad themselves checked out the toilets to see that they were empty as the police got the civilians out of the pub until only the squad was left inside. Of course they located the body immediately but stopped for a cigarette to waste the time that they were supposedly checking out the building. Equipment had been wheeled in that was really the means of getting the body out, and after ten minutes, declared the place clean and that it must have been a hoax call.

I had caused an awful lot of bother to the police, motorists, civilians as well as our own crowd, but Telford's body was spirited away and then dumped somewhere else to be found as though he'd fallen and crushed his throat and broke his neck at the same time.

His death wasn't even reported in the daily paper's the next day, it not being worthy of noting, but the bomb scare was. Jackson, I knew, would be furious, but there wasn't much I could do about that now, but this would be the following day.

It wasn't till we were quite some distance away did Lewis ask for more details though I countered with my own questions.

'How did that slime ball know I was supposed to be dead? I didn't think he had connections with the Middle East guys,' I said as we walked a couple of blocks before hailing a taxi to take us to his flat. I saw and noted the surprise on Lewis's face when I gave the cab driver his address.

'I know more than you think, Lewis, 'I said to the unspoken question I could see in his eyes as to my knowing where he lived. 'The point is, how did that shit know that I was supposed to be dead?' This stopped all questions and thoughts until we reached his flat.

'Why the fuck did you kill him?' was the first question from Lewis as he went and poured out a stiff drink for himself before pouring me one. 'We could have learned something!'

'I know, I know,' I said as I took my drink from him. 'It was the shock I think of seeing his shocked face at seeing me alive that made me react too quick. I tried to pull it back at the last moment but it was too late. Now keep my name out of this mess as I don't want to become involved because this might tip the hand of a person or persons unknown that I know that other people who shouldn't know that I am supposed to be dead. The whole bloody thing stinks,' I said, still not sitting down, but pacing up and down that short strip of carpet in his lounge. 'This Ba'athists group should be the only people who know, what with our news blanket on Nick's death. So how in God's name did he know?' I ranted.

'Well we're not going to know now, are we?' said Lewis laconically. 'You have seen to that.'

'Thanks for reminding me,' I said sardonically. 'Fuck it! The one good lead to start and I ball it up!'

I went and slumped in a chair and sipped at my drink. The fact that I had just killed a man didn't faze me at all, as I have said earlier that I have seen many dead bodies before, neglecting to mention that I had been the cause of their demise. This was just another one in a long line and had ceased to worry or even think about them afterwards. But I did with this one when we could have learned so much that I was really annoyed with myself.

'Maybe we can back track his movements?' Lewis offered.

'Join the queue on the M25, slowly moving but getting nowhere at all! Christ, he talks to everyone. It would take a month of Sundays.' With that, we slipped into a morose silence, each with his own thoughts. What Lewis's were, I don't know, but mine were running through all those people that I knew at the office, trying to think of who could be the mole and wanted me dead.

We didn't get anywhere that evening, talking as we ate frozen pizzas from the fridge. Cooked in the oven first, you cretin, and then I crashed out for the night on his sofa before going back to Toy Town.

Chapter Five

I caught an early train from London and at my station, took a taxi and had it drop me off at the pub where it was easy for him to turn the car round for his return journey. I just had time for a pint before the afternoon closure, getting to hear all the local news that only took ten minutes to tell. Of course, Nick's murder still being the top priority news and would be so for quite some time to come, I realised. But I did learn that a car had been parked in the pub's car park for quite some time since fairly early that morning and that I hadn't spotted it because of the drayman's vehicle blocking it from my view when he was making his delivery. Dave, the landlord, saying how he had told the police when he was questioned about strangers in Toy Town, of the two men driving off without so much as stopping for a drink. I might as well have asked that stupid parrot he had in the bar for a description of these men and would have most probably got a better answer than what he could give me.

Thanking him for the drink, I then went next door to our shop, somewhat dingy inside, noting that the windows could do with a good clean and then maybe it would be a bit lighter inside. Mrs. Morgan was there inside, a tired old woman of at least sixty years of age. She was a widow now, her husband having whisked her away from Wales to settle down here but died and left her to look after this little shop on her own. After a polite hello and discussion on her health and of that terrible event on the cliffs, did we get down to the purpose of my visit to her humble establishment. To save time, I wrote down a list of supplies that I wanted and said that I would take the milk with me and would come back just before she closed to pick up the rest.

'No bother to yourself, Mr. Farrell,' she replied. 'My niece is here and will bring it down when I get it ready,' she smiled. I thanked her and gave her twenty pounds and said to hold the change for when I came in the next time. I left with a carton of milk and walked down

Meadows Lane to my cottage which was under threat now as was my own life.

I loved the place having lived there now for four years and I was damned if someone was going to drive me out of it. I noted that the stables had delivered six bags of manure and I would deal with that after a nice cup of tea. So half an hour later, having had a cup and getting changed, dragged the bags round to the back and started to see to that part of the garden first.

It must have been close to seven o'clock and what with the low clouds, the light had started to fade from the sky when I straightened up and stretched my back. The female voice startled me in that peaceful idyllic setting and I turned round.

'I brought down your groceries, Mr. Farrell. I banged on the front door and, well, came round here,' said this lovely young woman holding a loaded box. I stuck my fork into the earth and went down towards her, noting that she was quite pretty, aged about twenty four, light brown hair and, when I got closer, light blue to green eyes. Her clothes were more of a social kind than countrified, a white blouse that looked nicely filled was tucked into a cream coloured skirt. Nicely shaped slender legs and noted that she wasn't wearing stockings with her flat heeled shoes of the same colour.

'Here, let me take that,' I said, reaching out for the box.

'Not with those dirty hands,' she smiled, turning away slightly. 'I'll bring them in while you wash,' she said, turning to the open doorway and going inside. Nice looking bum, too, I thought as I followed her inside the kitchen, turning on the light before going to the sink and turning on the tap. She placed the box on the table and turned to watch me.

'It's all there except the tomato ketchup. Ugh. How can you eat that stuff?' she said with her lilting Welsh accent.

'I only use it to add to my cooking. It's a bit softer than using tomato puree,' was all that I managed to say before one glass pane of the window shattered. I was halfway across the kitchen before I heard the report of the gun and took this young girl in a half rugby tackle to take us both crashing to the floor as a second pane shattered and the ceiling lamp exploded in a shower of glass.

I must say it was a soft landing for me with her being underneath, but not for her as her breath came out in one great whoosh as my weight expelled it from her body. I was panting in the half gloom as I felt her chest heave as she tried to take in air to breathe.

'Stay still,' I said somewhat too fiercely, but rolled off her as I suddenly felt myself begin to rise with having a soft body of a woman beneath me. I'm not a monk and not having any relations with a woman for some years was an unsettling experience there on my own kitchen floor. Whether she felt it, I don't know because I carried on rolling across the floor to reach up under the table where I had a gun taped. It was fully loaded and had been carefully oiled and knew that I felt much more comfortable with it in my hand. I strained my ears for any other outside noise and then asked her what her name was in a soft whisper.

'Mary,' came the same soft voice, 'Mary O'Sullivan.'

'Well, Mary O'Sullivan. Keep down and away from the window. Don't be frightened, but I've got to leave you here. I'll be back in a few minutes.' I heard her whispered protestations as I scuttled across the floor and into the parlour. Then I was up and out of the front door in a flash, running down out into the lane and down to the pebbled beach.

I'd surmised that the shots had come from a sniper's rifle and that the only place he could have been was on the little hill between the two lanes, so I was racing along the lower cliffs to get past there to come up behind them, if they were still there. I made my way up the slope keeping close to the ground and slowly made my way up the hill from the reverse slope. It was empty, but I found out where he, or she, had lain as the grass was still flattened out. I also found one of the cartridge cases that the would-be killer had obviously been unable to find in their haste to get away from being unable to do the job properly.

I put the spent casing in my pocket and then rolled over the top of the hill so as not to be silhouetted against the skyline before getting up and running down to my back garden.

'Mary. Mary O'Sullivan? Are you still in there and okay?' I called out in a low voice as I approached the open back door.

'Yes, and I'm frightened,' came the tremulous reply, but I still erred on the side of caution and went round to the front of the cottage. The front door was still open and I slid inside and went down onto my stomach and wormed my way across the parlour until I could put my head round the lower half of the door that led into the kitchen. With my eyes becoming accustomed to the gloom, could see that she was alone in the kitchen and cowering in the corner by the range.

I then got up and went over and helped her up and she clung to me, crushing those lovely breasts up against my chest and began to cry.

'Why was somebody trying to kill us?' she sobbed, her tears beginning to make my shirt wet.

'Not you, Mary O'Sullivan. Not you, but me,' I said softly, liking the feel of this young female holding me, feeling myself becoming aroused again.

'But why?' she countered.

'That I don't know,' I said, getting myself disentangled from her arms before she could really feel how her body had affected me and sitting her down in a chair. 'But they won't try again tonight. They've gone.'

'You were gone so long I thought they might have killed you and then come after me,' she continued, her cries now slowing down to the odd sob and hiccup.

'They're not after you. Rest assured on that fact. It's me they are after.'

'But why?' she asked, almost going off into a wail again.

'I don't know,' I said again, kneeling down and taking her hand in mine and beginning to rub it. 'But they will not try again tonight, believe me, I know. Maybe tomorrow, the day after or next month, I don't know, but I will find out. Now you've been very badly shaken up, would you like a drink?'

'Oh yes, please!' So I got up and went into the parlour and fixed her a strong vodka and tonic while I had a small one. I might still need my wits in spite of what I told her.

I gave her the drink of which she almost finished in one gulp as I fished out a lantern from one of the cupboards and primed it before I lit it. I then placed it near the window after pulling the curtains closed so that we would not be silhouetted by its light. Her face was white from the strain of the past half hour and so I refreshed her glass but refrained myself from having another.

'Tell you what,' I said, being all jovial now as I started to unpack the box of groceries that she had brought down. 'How about helping me eat something from this box of goodies?'

'I don't think I could eat anything now,' she said, still looking a little bit scared.

'Well, I could eat a horse after that bit of excitement,' I said.

'How could you after somebody has just tried to kill you?' she cried as I got out a couple of pans from the cupboard and put them on the stove.

'I'm still alive,' I said, waving a small frying pan at her, 'and that's why I'm hungry,' banging the pan down to emphasize the point.

'Let me do it then,' she said with a sniff as she got up from the chair. 'Let me get the condemned man his last meal,' moving across to me at the stove. 'It's the least I can do for him saving my life,' she said with a tired smile.

'That's better. You're smiling again, but condemned? Never! Okay. So what shall we have?'

'I'll cook you a Welsh omelette and then you'll never want any other omelette again.'

'Is it that bad?' I asked with a smile.

'Cretin!' she shouted, coming at me with the frying pan. 'I meant that it will spoil you for any other kind of omelette you might ever eat again.'

'I didn't mean it that way,' I cried as I stood up to fend off this wielded frying pan, catching her wrist and bringing her arm down as my other arm went round her. Why I kissed her there, then, at that point, I don't know, but she melted straight into my arms and returned my kiss with some passion.

'Oh you!' she then pushed me away, 'you're getting me all confused!' and I liked the way she blushed as she turned away to go back to the stove. I didn't say anything but sat down in the chair and wondered at that kiss. How sweet it tasted and that it had come in the heat of the moment and had been spontaneous and yet we had both, I think, responded to it. Well I did, that's why I had to sit down so that she wouldn't see that I had an erection inside of my trousers. It's very difficult to tell when a woman is aroused like you can with a man. But I think it was the blushing of her cheeks that told me she had liked the brief encounter and I wasn't sure if she would like it again for I damn well knew that I would.

While she bothered at the stove, I had to stay sitting down till I felt that my erection had subsided somewhat before getting up and making a quick and simple salad and cutting and buttering some bread as well as opening a bottle of wine. The omelette was delicious and I can honestly say that it was the best I have ever tasted. With the salad and wine, it was a lovely way to finish off an evening, well almost, considering the start that we'd had. I won't go into details now, but probably will later, but she insisted on washing up the dirty dishes before I escorted her back up the lane and deposited her at the shop door where she was staying with her aunt. I took a chance, and it was worth it, because I thanked her for a wonderful meal, apologising for the start as I took her in my arms and kissed her. Once again, having those lovely breasts crushed up against my chest and, rather reluctantly, released her so that she wouldn't feel that I was once again getting an erection at this bodily contact.

I sailed down the lane with the memory of her responding to my kiss and the almost promise that there might be more to come in the future. This being an almost saying that if I lived that long, but I didn't care. For the first time in my life I felt that I was in love and it would be to hell with the rest of the world if I couldn't take this romance a bit further.

I got undressed in my bedroom and got into bed and laid on my back as I thought of Mary, at the way she had returned my kisses. The feel of her breasts up against my chest and sure that she had felt my erection that had developed as I held her close to me. As hard as it was now in my hand and I gave out a groan as I slowly began to masturbate. I tried to picture her without any clothes on and that she was smiling at me and came towards me, her tits leading the way and that it was her that was now holding my cock. I tried then to think of her going down onto her knees and taking me into my mouth and....and that's when I came, shooting my load for it to splash all over my stomach and hand. It relieved the ache within my balls but not the one in my heart as I had to get up to clean myself off before getting back into bed to fall asleep dreaming of her.

***

Next morning, I went over the hill and down to Nick's cottage and as soon as I entered, knew that somebody else had been in there. It wasn't trashed, but I knew from previous visits that the place had been searched, turned over by a professional as it were. They were only minute details, but it was what I was trained at and knew what to look for and knew that I was good at my job. I knew that as I got older I would have to give up being an active agent in the field, if I lived that long though the present prospects didn't auger well for me; I would take over a training aspect, though I would rather have had the Arabian desk.

Now I knew that Jackson wasn't far off retirement and that he was training his successor to take over, who by chance, happened to be the man at the desk that I was coveting. It was a slim chance because usually when a desk became vacant, it went to the field officer of that region and us field men going to the back of the queue, though with my fluent command of many of the Arabian dialects, thought I might have a chance.

Be that as it may, I went back over the hill to my cottage only to find D.I. Loomis and D.C. Dawkins sitting at my kitchen table.

'Please forgive the intrusion, Mr. Farrell,' said Loomis, getting up and offering to shake hands, 'but we thought you'd like to know a bit more about what happened a little while ago in respect of the other Mr. Farrell.' I shook his hand and acknowledged the nod from Dawkins as Loomis sat back down and me taking another chair.

'On making our enquiries, we have reason to believe that the perpetrators on the attack on Mr. Farrell were of foreign extraction. They'd parked their car in the local public house's car park to do their business before leaving. Also that postman had been asked about where Mr. Farrell lived and he, being helpful, had told them. We also found a letter in his coat that was actually addressed to you, but he somehow had it in his pocket,' which he then produced and handed it to me. I took it and put it to one side. 'We have opened it, I'm afraid. It might have held some clue as to why he was killed. It didn't tell us anything, but, it appears that your postman does sometimes get confused when it comes to delivering the letters to a Mr. Farrell. Do you think that they might have picked on the wrong man?'

'Don't be ridiculous,' I said promptly and emphatically, hoping that they would go away from that line.

'Oh I don't think so,' he replied. 'You work for a certain room number, er….'

'Forty two,' supplied Dawkins.

'Yes, of the Foreign Office. Well, we might be country bumkins to those from London, but we can still add two and two otherwise we would be out of a job. Now there's not a lot we can do, Mr. Farrell, in respect of safeguarding your life, but I would say that you should take extreme caution in the future.'

If you only but knew that they had tried again only last night, was my thought then, but I didn't say anything. D.I. Loomis wasn't stupid either. Though I'd cleaned away the glass from the smashed panes of glass and of the ceiling light, it was still a glaring obviousness that something else had happened. Give him his due, he could see that I noticed that he had seen these small things and awaited my comment, but as I didn't give any, he gave a shrug to his shoulders and stood up.

'Take care, Mr Farrell. If we can be of help, do not hesitate to call us,' he said as he shook my hand before leaving.

That was my first surprise visit of the morning. The second one was when Mary O'Sullivan came knocking at my door.

'I saw the car with two men pull out from the lane and guessed they were the police, Mr Farrell. So I came down to find out what you told them about last night,' she said as she hovered in the doorway.

'Come in, Mary, and remember I told you last night that my name is Michael, or just plain Farrell. I was just about to make some lunch, would you care for some? I was only going to do a salad and cheese.'

'That would be lovely,' she said, coming into the cottage. 'Let me give you a hand. No. Tell you what. I'll do the salad and you can open a bottle of wine.' She was very bright and breezy compared to the tremulous girl of last night. I noted that her blouse was different and was sure that I could see her nipples pressing against the front and when she turned round couldn't see any outline of a bra strap across her back. She was wearing a white skirt this day, no stockings again, which made me wonder if she was wearing panties or not, and a pair of sandals instead of shoes. Also, she had put on a little make-up. Not a lot, but more just a hint to make her eyes seem a little larger, and lovely eyes they were.

She got the salad things out of the fridge and passed me a bottle of white wine from it to open.

'Well, what did they say about last night then?' she asked as she washed a tomato prior to cutting it.

'Nothing. I didn't tell them,' I replied, popping the cork and pouring out two glasses of the wine.

'What! We're shot at and nearly get killed and you didn't tell them? Then why were they here?' she asked somewhat hotly, accepting the glass of wine that I handed to her and taking a sip.

'They came to tell me of what they had learned in respect of the killing of Nicholas Farrell,' I answered.

'Mistaken identity! Last night proves that, I think.' Bright girl.

'It would appear so and I think that they also noticed the broken panes and smashed lamp. But as I didn't say anything, neither did they, but I think that is the conclusion that they have come to also.'

'Can you cut and butter some bread, I'm nearly finished here,' she asked going off on a tangent. This I did and we soon sat down to our light lunch. 'Now tell me more,' she said as she began to eat.

'No. Tell me about yourself first.'

'Well, that won't take long. I'm twenty four years of age and not very beautiful, and, oh come on! You're supposed to interrupt and say that I am!' she said with a grin.

'Oh, I'm sorry,' I said, coughing on the wine I had hastily gulped. 'Yes, you are wrong to say that you are not beautiful. Please accept my apologies,' I said grinning back at her, liking her sense of humour.

'Okay,' somewhat mollified. 'My father was Irish, hence the O'Sullivan and my mother Welsh. Glynis Jones and Megan Morgan being her sister, my aunt who runs the shop. I've just finished university and am having a year off for practical study before taking my Masters in Psychology. That's it, that's me. Oh, I've no other brothers or sisters either and have been spoilt rotten.' The last said with another grin that made me laugh because she had taken too much of a mouthful just before and she had a blob of mayonnaise stuck above her upper lip. I felt a sudden urge to lean across the table and lick it off for her but restrained myself and pointed it out. The tip of her tongue was so pink as it came out between her teeth to lick at it that I felt tremors run through my body at the lascivious way she looked at me as she did so, and wondered if I could get the tip of that tongue to move as it had, over the head of my cock. 'Now tell me about yourself.'

'I told you most of it last night,' I protested.

'But I had other things on my mind, like gunshots, wounding and maybe killing, so remind me.' I gave a sigh and recounted what I had once previously said to her.

'I come from a middle class family just outside of London. My mother died when I was thirteen after a long illness that took its toll on my father. That he loved her was painful to me to see him pine away and die two and half years later. I had a good education and learned French and German at school and came out top in both languages. It was during my last year at school that we had an Arabian boy there and he got me interested in Arabic and so I took to learning that one too. I also took an interest in the Middle East and learned an awful lot with his help as to the customs and beliefs of his country. I think I know as much of the Koran as I do of the Bible now. Anyway, after the death of my father, I'd finished school, I decided to join the Army.' We'd practically finished our meal here and the wine bottle was empty, so I opened another before continuing.

'The recruiting sergeant didn't want to know as I couldn't get my parents to sign the form. What about your guardian, he asked of me after producing the death certificates of my mother and father. You be my guardian then, I said to him and you can then sign the form for me. Against all the rules and regulations and with a twinkle in his eye did just that and signed the form for me.

'So at not quite sixteen, I joined the army in the boys division. I did well and was made up to sergeant before I was eighteen when I then transferred into the regular army, but had to drop back to corporal. Within three months I was a sergeant again and kept breaking the one rule that all soldiers are taught when they join. Never volunteer! I volunteered for everything, being it catering, guard duty whatever. It didn't do me any harm and it got me noticed. It was when we were doing a tour of duty in Germany that they really found out that I was fluent in that language and kept getting shifted from post to post to help out in the translations. It also came out about my knowing French and Arabic that I got pulled out and sent to the War Office in London. There I had to sign the Official Secrets Act and it has since led me up to where I am now. More than that, I cannot tell you.'

What I did not, or could not say, was that I then began to be sent undercover to infiltrate the illegal immigration system that was operating and pose as a prospective immigrant myself. I could speak the gutter language and just after a few hours in the sun, looked just the same colour as the rest of them. I paid my money, provided by the British Government and would get shipped to England with a load of other would be hopefuls that we would get visas. My job was to ascertain who were genuine and who were or looked to be potential terrorists. I got many sent back and only came to the attention of Jackson after I had killed two of them.

'He pulled me out of that system to put me into his and gave me to the care of Lewis. He took me through all the nuances of the Arabian desk and became my field officer when I was sent out to become an assassin. That was four years ago and now I was in a situation where somebody wanted me dead and I was going to do my damndest to stay alive until I knew who it was.'

But this was what I couldn't tell this Mary O'Sullivan and we'd now finished lunch and the second bottle of wine and so she made some coffee which we took into the parlour and sat on the settee to drink. Now I'm blaming the wine and the fact that I had this beautiful woman sitting next to me that made me act as I did. With the coffee finished and we sat there in our own thoughts, mine being those that I had in bed the night before, that I leaned over and took her into my arms and kissed her. She too must take some blame because she responded to my advances and before we knew it, I had her blouse open and had my hand on a tit, rubbing it and making the nipple rise up as hard as a nut. Her hands had undone the buttons of my shirt and her hands were moving over my back and chest, lightly scratching me with her nails as she gave out a low moan at what I was doing. For I had now moved down a little to not only kiss those lovely breasts and nibble on the nipples, but to also get my rampant cock into a more comfortable position.

It was when I was trying to get her skirt off of her body, she lifted herself up to help and it was with this movement of hers that made us both roll off the settee and onto the rug on the floor. We both gurgled at this and I just loved the way her breasts moved at this and she kept the grin on her face as I managed to get her skirt off and found that she wasn't wearing any panties after all.

I had to stand up to get my trousers off as she sat up and took off her blouse. Her eyes didn't leave off looking at me and her smile got even wider when my erection sprang free from my trousers as they came down. I had to sit down on the settee for a moment to get them off from my feet, my erection really throbbing now at the prospect of putting it inside that beautiful body that was now spread out on the rug before me. I stood up, my cock swinging from side to side as I stepped in between her legs that she'd just opened for me and I went down onto my knees between them.

The fact that I made a complete mess of our first coupling I could only put it down to the fact that I hadn't been with a woman for nearly four years and was just too eager. I had moved over her and it was when the head of my cock came in contact with her pubic hairs that I came. Shooting my seed all up her thigh and lower stomach. I gave out a cry of dismay for I was still moving my body down onto hers as I tried to stop my ejaculation as my stomach came down onto hers, squashing my still throbbing and spurting out cock between us.

Mary wasn't a virgin and accepted my apologies at my over eagerness that I had made a mess between our two bodies and crooned as she held me and said that it was all right and it would be perfect a bit later on once I'd regained, or remade what I had just lost. And she was right for with her using not only her hand, but taking me into her mouth helped raise me up again. It was a wonderful sight to see her breasts swing about as she knelt between my legs and had those lovely lips clamped round the head of my prick as she sucked on me.

It was an hour later from my first attempt that she deemed it was up hard enough for her to release me from that inner heat of her mouth for me to use it properly. So she moved and lay down beside me and I rolled over onto my side and kissed her first, not minding that those lips had been on my cock, for they were still nice to kiss. My cock was now up hard again and I got between her legs and looked down at my target and looked up to see her smile and with her arms open, I moved over on and entered both her body and arms. So we coupled and it resulted in us both having an experience that would be most memorable.

She had sucked me into that heat of her body, her legs coming up by my sides as I stretched myself over her till I could go no further. I lifted myself up onto my elbows but still had the nipples of her breasts touching my chest as I began to move myself in and out of this wonderful woman beneath me.

I was disappointed in myself by not being able to bring her to an orgasm this first time, but it was my fault for still being too keen to fuck her and came within a few minutes of being inside this darling woman.

Dusk was falling when we, after a final kiss and grope, roused ourselves up and went upstairs and had a shower. I wish that the shower cubicle had been bigger for both of us to be inside at the same time, for I would just have loved to have had the pleasure of soaping her. As it was, all I could was help rub her down with a towel before having my shower.

With that finished, I put on a dressing gown and went downstairs to find her looking slightly ridiculous in one of my oversized dressing gowns as she made us dinner. With this we had another two bottles of wine, red this time, and then went up to my bedroom where she stayed the night to try and compliment what had happened during the afternoon.

We went into my bedroom and when inside, she turned to face me, a lovely smile on her face as we went into an embrace and kissed. We both moved at the same time to push the dressing gowns off each other's shoulders and they fell unheeded to the floor as we moved close together again. My erection getting squashed between us as we held each other tight.

It only took a little push for her to fall back onto the bed, breaking the contact between us. Words were not needed for she said it all in the smile that she gave me as her arms opened as did her legs and I moved in between both of them. Sliding up into her again was heaven to me as her arms closed over round my shoulders.

'Oh darling,' she breathed as she felt my hardness moving up inside her. I lay on her front and kissed her as my chest squashed her breasts before lifting myself up to start moving my hips as I began to fuck her. This time I was able to hold that little bit longer than before and soon had her thrashing about under me as I kept humping myself and came at the same time as she did.

She gave out a little cry as I pulled out and lay down on my side next to her. Sated and happy at having this beautiful woman nestling in the crook of my arm with her free hand running up and down the sparse hairs of my chest, I asked what would her aunt think?

'She won't know whether I'm in or out,' she said sleepily, 'besides, I don't want to leave,' which made my heart leap.

'Nor do I want you to go, Mary O'Sullivan,' I said softly as I kissed her hair and began to stroke her naked breast. 'I think I've fallen in love with you.'

'I bet you say that to all the women,' she said and I could hear the smile in her voice.

'The only other woman I've said that to was my mother, and I think she would have approved of you,' I said, still stroking her.

'Oooh, don't stop talking. Just keeping saying how much you love me,' she crooned, so I did which resulted in us coming together again.

Chapter Six

Love or sex must have dulled my senses because I didn't even hear or feel her leave the bed the next morning. It was my sense of smell that woke me, the aroma of coffee being brewed what finally got me up. It was an alarming thought that I, or we, could have been taken that night and it made me resolve to myself that I mustn't be led along this path of false security. I wasn't out of danger by any means and I must keep my guard up at all times. This resolve almost disappeared when I got downstairs wearing my dressing gown to find her at the stove wearing one of my shirts with only one button done up.

'Oh my God!' I said as I slumped down in a chair at the table seeing at how she was dressed and what I could see of her body. The lower cheeks of her pretty bum peeking out from the tail end of the shirt. 'What a sight to greet a man first thing in the morning.'

'What's wrong?' she asked, looking slightly alarmed as she put down a coffee mug on the table beside me, one breast almost coming out to greet me.

'Nothing. That's the problem,' I said as I caught her arm and pulled her down to sit on my lap, squashing the erection that I had gotten at seeing her like this. 'You look absolutely gorgeous and desirable compared to how I feel,' I said, giving her a kiss, not failing to notice that her ample breasts were fully in my sights.

'You might be a bit stubbly round the chin, but you look gorgeous too,' she said, kissing me again. 'Now how about breakfast,' she asked sprightly as she got up from my lap, feeling, I think, that I had reacted to the closeness of her body.

'Nothing would be better than to see you cook me a breakfast,' I replied, and it was nice as I said, to see her in my shirt prepare the breakfast and I counted myself a lucky man to have found such a treasure. But her beauty and the knowing pleasure of her body didn't prevent me from looking at my plate and devouring everything that had been placed upon it.

'My darling Mary, that was the most wonderful breakfast I've ever had,' I said as I finished my second cup of coffee.

'Oh Michael,' she exclaimed as she came and sat on my lap again. 'That's the first time you've called me darling!'

'No it isn't! I called you that last night, or was it in the afternoon?' I protested.

'You didn't use the word!' she argued, wiggling her bottom on my lap which was most discomforting, 'but let's not our first morning together start, or finish with an argument. I love you, Michael Farrell, and I hope that you love me as much as I have come to love you in these two short days.'

'I think I fell in love with you when I first saw you holding that box of groceries,' I said giving her a kiss on the cheek, her not seeming to mind that I'd slipped my hand into the shirt and was fondling the tit that I'd found inside.

'I think I did too in spite of the fact that your hands were covered with horse manure,' she smiled, turning her head down and kissing me on the lips. 'Ugh! Go upstairs and shave or grow a beard for it scratches,' she said, getting up off my lap. 'But there again, a moustache might tickle me in the right places,' she finished with a wicked grin.

'You hussy,' I said as I smacked her bare bottom that was quite visible beneath the shirt she was wearing as I got up. I went upstairs and showered and shaved before getting dressed and going back downstairs again. Mary had just finished cleaning up the kitchen and looked more than desirable in my shirt than I would have thought possible.

'Michael, you're in a suit!' she exclaimed as I took her into my arms and kissed her.

'Yes, my sweet. I've got to go to London. I made a mistake last night.'

'Last night!' she exploded. 'Last night!' and I could see that her breasts were quivering in what could be anger or rage.

'Darling, darling let me explain,' trying to hold her still from the sudden anger that what I had said had aroused. 'Not you, not you, but me. I let my guard down and could have been taken. Not just me, but you too! I love you and now I have to be doubly careful not only for myself but you also. Oh Mary O'Sullivan,' I said as I took her into my arms and held her very tight to my body, 'I didn't think this could happen to me at this worst moment of my life when someone is trying to kill me. I love you and don't want anything ever to happen to you because of me. I've got to go to London to try and sort out who that person is and I want you to get back up to your aunt's and stay there. Do not! Do not stay here in the cottage. Believe me, it's the best you can do.'

'When will you be back?' she asked, the tears that had begun to form when I first spoke were now running down her cheeks.

'As soon as I can, my darling, but do as I say and go back to your aunt's and stay there,' I said, kissing her wet cheeks, tasting the salt and had to fight to keep the tears back from my own eyes. 'Now I've found you, I don't want to lose you.' My voice was now choked with emotion as we clung to each other in mutual support. We finally broke apart and she went and got dressed while I phoned for a taxi to meet me at the pub.

'If you are planning on staying here for awhile,' I started as we went up the lane together.

'Which I most definitely am,' she interrupted.

'You had better see to having a few more supplies laid in at the cottage,' I said with a smile and gave her a kiss out of view of the shop. 'I'll be back as soon as I can,' I promised, as our hands slowly parted and she went to the shop and I to the waiting taxi.

I had to hang around the station for nearly an hour before the London train came in, and by the time I got to the London terminal it was evening. I took another taxi and had him drop me off at the corner of the road where Lewis lived. I wanted to keep a low profile so I thought I would spend the night at his place. There was no answer to the door bell so after ten seconds, I had the door open and was safely inside, there not being many locks that I couldn't open. I made myself a snack from his fridge and settled down to watch television till he came home which wasn't until after the pub's had closed.

'What the fuck are you doing here?' was the greeting I got when he walked into his lounge to find me sitting there.

'Why do you always greet me with the same words?' I countered, not bothering to get up. 'I thought you might be pleased to see that I'm still in the land of the living.' Something made me stop from going any further. The less everyone knew that another attempt had been made on my life, the better off I might be. 'I thought I'd pop in to see what was happening to the rest of the world,' I said flippantly.

'Bugger all,' was his reply as he went and got himself a drink. 'So why are you here now?' he asked as he settled himself in a chair with his drink in his hand.

'Well the first is, you don't mind if I doss down here for awhile? I don't want to advertise my presence in London and have another Telford problem.'

'Telford!' he snorted. 'I got one awful bollocking from Jackson over that. Do you know we tied up a quarter of the Met. Police force over that bomb scare. Fuck, did he ream me! You'll get the same when he sees you.'

'That I expect when I go to the office tomorrow, but I'm asking about tonight? Can I doss down here?'

'Of course you can. But you make your own breakfast.'

'Fine, thanks. So if I can have a blanket, I'll do just that.' So he got me a couple of blankets and a pillow and I didn't have a bad night's sleep considering.

***

Next morning I went to the office and spent nearly an hour at the Middle East desk, reading Arabic papers to keep up with the news in that part of the world before Jackson learned that I was in the building. Up to his office I went and got the expected bollocking over the Telford escapade.

'Why?' was the only question he asked after the reaming out he gave me, and I went on to explain in answer to his question. He listened and then, grudgingly, admitted that my theory that I was being set up sounded logical and that Telford had confirmed it. That I killed the man was bye the bye now. It had happened, much to both our regrets, because we might have been able to get something out of the man.

'Well, who are those you suspect and who are those you have ruled out?' Jackson asked of me.

'Well, I ruled you out first, sir,' I said.

'Well, thank you for that, and what if I had been suspected?'

'We wouldn't be talking now,' I said succinctly. 'You've nothing to gain by having me put away. Likewise Lewis. He has had many chances to drop me in the shit in the field, but I'm still here. From there on, I think of everybody else as suspect.'

'You can rule out Jane too,' he said absent mindedly as he looked as though he was deep in thought. Jane Merryweather was his secretary and knew more about everybody than anyone and I had to agree with this so I crossed her off my mental list. We both sat there for some time thinking our own thoughts, mine running through all the people who knew me in the building and came up with too many.

Then I remembered the letter that Nick had in his pocket for me and was now in mine. Would that hold a clue? I quickly got it out and opened it from the envelope to find it was an internal memo saying that I was overdue for my yearly medical, so it wasn't because of that. I dropped it on the desk and Jackson picked it up and read it.

'Hmm, well, as you're here now. Jane?' he said into the phone when she answered hers. 'I've got Farrell in here and he needs his physical. Can you get it fixed up please? Thank you.' He replaced the phone and we then ran over a few names to try and sort the wheat from the chaff without coming to any conclusions. The phone rang and he answered it and just grunted before replacing the receiver. 'Two o'clock tomorrow afternoon, usual place,' he said to me. 'So where are you staying for the night?' I hesitated for a moment before replying.

'Lewis's place.' His eyebrows lifted.

'I didn't know you knew where he lived.'

'Neither did he,' I grinned, 'until I turned up the other day.'

We talked a bit more before I went downstairs to where the desks were and saw Lewis at the International desk talking to Fergie whose desk it was. I told him of my appointment and asked if he didn't mind me staying another night on his sofa.

'No problem,' he replied. 'So what will you do all day till then?'

'Catch up on the news over there,' indicating the Middle East desk. 'Have my examination and then go home from there.' That was okay by him, and so I left him in his flat the next morning and went to the office and spent the morning reading all the latest news, noting that more trouble was brewing up again in Iran and Iraq.

There must be something about the doctors of Harley Street, for every time I've gone for my physical there has been a different nurse on duty. They have all been young and attractive and I didn't mind the slightest in her being in the room with the doctor when I did finally strip off my last piece of clothing. I was passed fit and before I left the sumptuous office, she smiled at me and gave me her phone number. If I hadn't just met Mary O'Sullivan, I might have stayed in London for a bit longer, but I was now eager to get back home.

It was nearly nine o'clock when the taxi dropped me off outside the pub, but instead of going in, went and knocked on the closed door of the shop. It was several minutes before a light came on and the door was opened. It was a pleasure to see her face light up with that smile and came out and kissed me.

'I've missed you,' she said in her lilting voice as she held me.

'I've missed you too,' I replied, giving her another kiss. 'Do you think you can slip out for a drink and….'

'Yes,' she answered instantly. 'Wait here, I'll just tell aunt that I'm going out.'

She quickly went back into the shop and a few minutes later was back out with her coat on. She closed the door to the shop and it made me ask about her keys to get back in.

'I won't need the keys,' she grinned wickedly at me. 'Aunt will have the shop open by the time I get back.' I gave her a hug and we went into the pub and ordered a drink. It was Dave the landlord who served me with our second drink and then leaned on the bar so that he could speak softly to me.

'You remember I told you about that car that was on the car park the other week?' I said that I did. 'Well, another strange car has been seen, but it didn't stop here. It was parked up outside your cottage for about an hour today.'

'What time was this?' I asked, my heart thumping and all kinds of bells jangling inside my head.

'Around lunch time. Old George,' a neighbour of mine, 'came in late and told me, just before closing time.'

'Did he see who it was?'

'No. With his bad eyes he just said that it was a man he'd not seen before.'

'Well, thanks, Dave,' I said as I then took our drinks back to where Mary was and sat down deep in thought.

'Penny for them,' she said as she sipped at her gin and tonic.

'They're not worth that much. I wish you'd brought the keys to the shop with you.'

'Why?'

'Because you're not coming down to the cottage tonight.'

'Why?' her face taking on a strained look.

'Somebody's been inside there today and I have a nasty suspicion that it's not a very safe place for you to visit.'

'Oh, Michael Farrell! I've been inside and been shot at and now you're telling me it's not a safe place. Well, I'm coming down there with you whatever you say.' Her Irish blood was up and we sat there for at least ten minutes arguing but I eventually gave up on the promise that she would stay some distance away while I went inside to check it out.

We finished our drinks and I borrowed a torch from Dave and we went down the lane to my cottage. I led her round the back in the dark and took her down to where the compost heap was and made her sit behind it.

Chapter Seven

I hadn't as yet replaced the two broken panes of glass in the kitchen window, so this was where I headed for with my torch on. I carefully checked all round the frame both inside and out before putting my hand through and opening the window to climb in. Crouched on the sill, I swept the torch around to make sure the floor was clear before lightly jumping down and kept down close to the floor. I had an idea what I was looking for and soon found it. A thin piece of wire had been taped across the bottom of the door that would have snapped at it being opened. I followed the wire along the skirting board to where it disappeared into a bottom drawer, which I then gently eased open. Inside was a nice little package that the wire went into and found that it was connected to a ten-second fuse that would set the bomb off and blow the kitchen and whoever was in it into smithereens.

I carefully removed the fuse and then pulled the wire out, making the whole thing safe. There must have been at least half a pound of Semtex in the package, but this had been wired to the back door. What about the front door? I could have walked in through that door and found the kitchen door wired. So if there was another bomb connected elsewhere and I snapped the wire, I would have just under ten seconds to get out, so I left the back door wide open in case.

I didn't dare touch the light switches but had to rely on the illumination of the torch to sweep ahead of me as I cautiously made my way to the front door. I found that my assumption was right, for this too had been wired in the same way with another half pound of Semtex. This I disconnected and got back into the kitchen and made another careful check around the cupboards. I couldn't bring Mary into the cottage in case there were any more planted around the place.

With the outside of my food cupboard checked, I opened it and pulled out enough food for us to eat supper and put them in my pockets. I shut the kitchen window and then went out and for the first time since I'd lived there, locked the kitchen door from the outside and put the key in a safe place.

'Oh, Michael,' came Mary's voice from the darkened garden, and she came rushing into the beam of my torch and flung her arms round me. 'You were in there so long I was getting worried.' I could taste the salt of her tears as she kissed me and this made my heart give another lurch at the thought that she really loved me and this began to make my cock rise.

'Sorry about that,' I said as I held and kissed her back. 'But we can't stay here the night.'

'We can go back to the shop,' she said, but I had a better idea. Now who said that a man could always be led by his prick? Well, this was certainly the case for I now had a really throbbing hard on inside my trousers.

'No. Come with me,' and I took her hand and led her out onto the cliffs. Here we walked hand in hand up over the hill and down to Nick's cottage. The back door was still unlocked and we went inside and I turned the light on.

'Well, it's a bit dusty but it's almost the same as yours. Whose place is this?' Mary asked.

'It belongs, no, belonged to Nick. Nick Farrell, the Farrell who got killed instead of me,' I replied, emptying my pockets of the food from my cupboard onto the table.

'Oh,' she said. 'Now tell me why we couldn't stay at your place?' I had refused to tell her as we had walked across the hill and so as I got plates out for supper, told her of the bombs.

'There might have been more than the two, so I didn't think it wise to try and find any more in the dark.'

'Oh Michael,' she cried coming into my arms again, a response that I was getting to rather like for after getting my dick to shrink back to its normal state on the walk over the hill, now started to rise up again. 'What if they are still out there? Shouldn't we turn the light off?'

'No,' I laughed. 'We're safe for the night. The person who planted them had a car and will be well away from here by now.'

'Michael, I don't want to lose you now after only just having found you,' tears coming to her eyes as she kissed me fiercely, now rubbing the front of her body up against mine, feeling, I'm sure, what was now being squashed.

'I don't want to lose you, Mary O'Sullivan, either, but there's a chance I might die of hunger first if you don't start fixing us something to eat,' I said after her kisses, getting her arms off from round me. 'It will have to be beer I'm afraid. I didn't want to open my fridge for the milk so I didn't bother bringing over the coffee.'

'Beer'll do fine,' she laughed and began to sort out what I'd brought to make us a meal. While she was doing this, I phoned the office and eventually got patched through to Jackson.

'There's been another attempt,' I said without preamble, and went on to tell him what I had found.

'I'll get a bomb squad down there right away,' he said when I'd finished talking.

'No. Please don't do that yet. The place is secure for the night and besides, it'll be better for them to turn the place over in daylight. Also I'd rather it be done without fanfare as I don't want to get the village up into a state of hysteria because of my being here.' I then told him where the key to the back door was as I didn't want them breaking it down to get inside.

'Okay. I'll have them down there at first light. Just keep out of sight and I'll phone you when they've finished and give you the details. Keep your head down because whoever is behind this will try again when they learn that they have failed again.' I told him I would and finished the call and went and opened two bottles of beer for us to have with the meal that was now ready.

'Michael?' Mary spoke as we held hands across the table, our beer glasses between us. Her eyes so soft and full of desire that it made me wonder if mine looked the same as I think that the same thoughts were running through her mind as were what was in mine. 'Are we staying here for the night?'

'If you want to, darling,' I said, squeezing her hand.

'That's settled then. Take me to bed and tell me how much you love me,' a sweet smile coming to her face. But with the bed last being used by Nick and that was several weeks ago, Mary stripped it while I found his linen closet and gave her clean sheets to remake the bed for us. Then we moved towards each other and slowly began to take each other's clothes off, me marvelling at the glorious body I was revealing that was mine for the night. This was between kisses before getting into bed and making glorious love to one another.

The start was for me to move down in between her open legs and use my mouth and tongue which caused her to give out a groan and have her body give a shiver.

'Together, Michael,' I heard her cry out. 'Together. Turn round.' I stopped licking her insides and turned my body on the bed and rolled over onto my back for her to get astride of me. It was lovely to have the nipples of her breasts stroke from the chest down to rest on my stomach as I felt her hand take hold of my erection and hold it upright.

Her hot breath over the head made it twitch and she stopped this by taking it into her mouth. What a glorious feeling to have her tongue rove over the partly exposed head, pushing the foreskin down to be able to suck on the bare flesh. While doing this, her leg had gone across my body and had both down by the sides of my chest as she lowered herself down for me to stick my tongue back up inside her.

With us doing this to each other, it wasn't long before she was squirming above me and I felt her body shake and felt her orgasmic juices start to flow down into my mouth. Her mouth was then filled with my sperm as I bucked my hips up, trying to get more of myself into her in this fashion. But she held the base of my cock firm so that I wouldn't choke her.

The cool air wafted round the head of my cock when she released me from the heat of her mouth as she licked round the exposed head before giving a sigh and moved off of me. Even though my mouth was wet from her juices, she still kissed me and licked round my face where I was still wet.

We kissed, held and stroked each other till I was roused up again and this time she lay on her back for me to enter her in the usual sexual position. We both lasted much longer this time until I gave out a groan and couldn't hold myself back any longer and came inside her. It was only by moving down again using my tongue was I able to bring her to her second orgasm.

I didn't get much sleep that night, not because of my love making with Mary, but because I couldn't close my mind down about the bombs in my own cottage. I was up early and leaving Mary in bed, went up the hill and lay in the still wet grass from the dew to look down at the cottage. I could see that the back door was open and knew that the squad were going over the place with a fine toothcomb. I couldn't see what vehicle they had come in but guessed it would be a rather nondescript thing that wouldn't cause any distress to the neighbours. After watching for a bit and seeing people moving about in one of the upstairs bedrooms, did I return to Nick's place to find Mary cobbling some sort of breakfast together for us. With no milk, it had to be tea au natural until we went up to the shop. She had found a shirt of Nick's that was a bit on the small side for her and I kept getting tantalising glimpses of her bare bum and muff that got me into such a state that as soon as we had eaten, we went back to bed again.

It was well past noon after a lovely morning of fucking each other that we finally got up and got dressed and I suggested that we have lunch in the pub before we got some supplies in or my cottage was declared free of any unwanted devices. Mary agreed to this and so we strolled up the lane, arm in arm and went into the pub. She insisted on popping next door to the shop first for some clean clothes and for me to order her lunch as she would not be long.

I'd only just given my order for drinks when Dave came up from the cellar, and espying me, beckoned me to the far end of the bar.

'I don't want to alarm you, Mr Farrell, but there's a van down the lane and there are some men in your cottage,' he whispered conspiratorially.

'Thanks for keeping an eye out, Dave, but I called them in. They are doing some work inside for me though I should have told you first so as not to cause concern but thanks all the same.'

'Think nothing of it. Got to keep an eye out for my regulars. There's not many of them so I got to try and keep them, haven't I?' he laughed. 'I'm what you might call the neighbourhood thing.'

'Watch,' I supplied.

'That's the word. Neighbourhood watch! Can't have strangers wandering around village what with many a door unlocked eh?'

'Perfectly right,' I agreed and then ordered lunch for two. I turned when the door of the pub opened and I saw Mary silhouetted against the sun, her slim legs clearly visible through the thin muslin type frock she was wearing. The sight made me want to forget lunch and take her back to the cottage again. I did say that Mary was the first woman I had known for nearly four years and now I couldn't get enough of her.

Her smile was bright as she came in and took the proffered drink, blowing me a silent kiss that gave my heart a nice kick and had to stifle the urge to take her into my arms there and then in the pub. She went and sat down with her back to the window and I liked the way the sun made her hair shine in many different shades of brown. Dave brought out our platters of food which what is known as a ploughman's lunch. Fresh bread with hunks of cheese and pickles and it really did look good enough to eat.

After finishing each tiny morsel after our meagre breakfast, feeling very content with a full satisfied stomach and a lovely woman to look at, felt at peace in body, but not in mind. I had the premonition that the phone would soon ring and was prepared for it when it did ring. I made the excuse that the reception would be better outside and quickly went out and answered it, knowing that it would be Jackson with some news.

'You did right staying out of the cottage for the night,' he said without preamble. 'They found another one that I think you might have missed in the dark. A pressure switch under the carpet on the upstairs landing about two foot in from the top of the stairs. The wire went along under the carpet and this one didn't have a time fuse, so you might not have spotted it in the dark. Well done, Michael!'

Then another thought hit me as he said this. Was this some kind of test of my abilities? Was it really Semtex or dummy bombs set up by Jackson to see if I was still fit for the field? Maybe he took advantage of the death of Nick to set up these traps and that the gun shots at the cottage were meant to miss? Would he go to those lengths to check me out? I doubted it, but it was something else to consider and so I now had to think of what to do to counter any more tricks to either prove my worth or prevent me being killed if the threat was real.

'Well, pass on my thanks to the boys and tell them that I'll stand them a good shout down at some pub when I'm back up in London. It will be all right for me to stay down here for awhile?' I asked. The answer was in the affirmative but said that I should still be on my guard while he looked into things from his end.

I went back to Mary and bought another drink for us both as I pondered as to what to do. She pre-empted me in one course of action when I sat down with our fresh drinks and told her that the cottage was now clear for us to use.

'That's good, because I was thinking while you were outside leaving me here all alone, again.' She stressed the last word. 'I'm moving in to look after you while you look after me.'

'You can't,' I blurted out. 'I'm still in danger!'

'Are you saying that you don't love me?' she cried, tears coming to her eyes.

'Mary darling. I love you with all my heart but I don't want you to get hurt while I've still got this problem to sort out,' I told her, taking her hand and rubbing it. 'I can't do my job properly to protect myself let alone putting you at risk too!'

'Michael Farrell! If anything happened to you, I'd die. So I'd rather die with you than without you!' Tears were now running down her face and I was glad that there were only two other people in the bar and were too far away to hear us.

'Mary O'Sullivan. I've come to love you more than life itself and I don't want to lose you. Can't you see that I'm still in danger and I don't want to get you involved.'

'But I am involved now. I love you and if whoever is doing this succeeds, I'd rather be with you than have to bury you.' Her tears had now become sobs and then her eyes began streaming tears and it took me quite some time, moving round and sitting beside her, holding her tight and, much to my reluctance, giving in to her wishes.

When she was composed and more her normal self, we finished our drinks and went next door to the shop to see her aunt for supplies for the cottage. I let Mary choose what we needed and when all was got together, I paid the bill and we went down to the lane to my now swept clean cottage.

I found the key in the same place that I had put it and we went into the kitchen and began putting away the food. We spent a pleasant afternoon on the settee, talking in between kisses and of us having sex again, learning more about each other and then found that night had fallen. I'd rigged up a storm lantern in the kitchen and she positively glowed under its soft light as she prepared dinner for us and as I sat there to watch her, realised how lucky I was to have found such a girl down here in my own back yard as it were. I cannot remember what the meal was but it went down very well with a bottle of wine and we were soon in bed to show each other at just how much in such a short time, we had come to have this love between us.

Going into the sixty nine position first as a prelude to me turning round and entering that lovely heat of her inside body. I loved that smooth and silky feel of her vagina that my cock moved in, feeling her internal muscles flexing all along the length of my shaft. Then to have her legs grip me tight across my waist and back as she began her orgasm. Bucking me about on top, striving to stay there, not being able to push myself harder into her as she screamed and let go of her orgasm. This triggered me to send out my seed and had the fleeting hope that she was taking the pill, but it was somewhat a bit late to be thinking of that at this time. It wasn't till after we had fucked for the second time that we finally, exhausted, fell asleep in each other's arms.

It was in the early hours of the morning when I shot bolt upright in bed, cursing myself for being a fool. Whoever had planted the bombs would know that they hadn't gone off and that I was still alive and, as I was now, probably back in the cottage, a sitting target for another attack. Needless to say that I didn't sleep any more that night, but had gone downstairs and sat there till it was full daylight expecting, but thankful, that no such attack came.

So for a change, I cooked breakfast and told Mary what I planned to do. She agreed, and after getting dressed, took some of our supplies and went off to the shop, only to make her way later down to Nick's cottage. While she was out, I rummaged around through my tools and other bits and pieces I had picked up over time and came up with two timing clocks. One I wired up to the kitchen and parlour light and timed it to come on when dusk fell and then go off later in the late evening. Then the other clock would kick in which was wired to the bedroom to come on as the downstairs lights went off, stay on for about twenty minutes and then switch off. This would then seem that we were inside and went up to bed at about a quarter to twelve. With this all wired up and tested, I then made my way across the hill to Nick's cottage where I planned to stay.

Chapter Eight

It was on the second night that an intruder came in. The first night had been perfect not only in not being interrupted, but that Mary and I got that much better acquainted as they say. Read that as sex, sex and more sex. Now instead of using the master bedroom, if you could call it that, his cottage being an almost replica of mine. The first bedroom at the top of the stairs was the larger and had a double bed in it. The spare, or second room, was a bit smaller and the bed wasn't as big, which was where I had placed us. In the big bedroom I had dummied up the bed so that it looked like that there were two people sleeping in there, and with the lights out, looked pretty much as I thought it would. We then slept in the other room but I made a point of having both doors kept open.

On this second night we'd gone to bed as usual and after our foreplay, made love, me coming twice and her having two orgasms before we eventually drifted off to sleep. Being a field operative and knowing that my life was being threatened, slept on a knife edge and came awake in an instant. Fully alert knowing that my brain had heard something out of the ordinary for the cottage we were sleeping in. I leaned up and put my hand over Mary's mouth to stop any sound as she came awake at my touch. Her eyes wide at the fact that I had covered her mouth with my hand.

'Don't make a sound,' I whispered into her ear. 'Whatever you do, keep quiet. Now slowly and quietly, roll out of bed and get on the floor and stay there. No noise or sound. Do you understand?' She nodded, her eyes now wide with fright. 'Good girl, and stay there till I call and say that all is clear.' I let go off her mouth and rolled over to my side of the bed and taking my gun, already cocked, from under my pillow, eased myself out of bed and onto the floor. I must say that Mary acted like a pro. I saw her move off the bed on the other side but didn't hear a sound as she disappeared from view to the floor.

Staying on the floor, I eased my way to our open door and out onto the landing. It was dark and there was only just the slight change in this darkness coming from the window of the other bedroom. I kept my breathing low and as normal as possible as I lay there on the carpet, trying to hear again whatever it was that woke me up.

It was only slight, but I heard that whisper of carpet of a foot not being raised high enough to prevent the brush of a foot across the pile. Someone was coming up the stairs but I still couldn't see anything in the darkness until they reached the open door of the other bedroom. Then I saw the dim outline of an outstretched arm that pointed inside and the sudden sound of the muted phut's of a silenced gun sending four shots into the dummied bodies in the bed there.

Two maybe three shots left in that gun, was my instant thought if he had one extra up the spout, as I fired off two shots. The sound so loud that it was deafening in the confined hallway as the noise rolled into one reverberating roll of thunder. There was a muted cry that told me I had hit my target that then made itself known by falling back down the stairs that led into the parlour.

Still keeping down, I made my way to the top of the stairs to see a figure lying down on the carpet almost in the middle of the room. I moved cautiously seeing that it wasn't moving and began to descend to the parlour when I saw the pale glimmer of a hand move. It was the one with a gun in it and I could see the muzzle flash but no sound as the bullet took me in the left upper arm, spinning me round to fall to my knees, feeling sick at the pain.

It was a snap shot that I took and had the pleasure of hearing the zing as it hit the gun in that hand and see it fly off into the gloom of the room. There was also the cry of pain as it was wrenched from that hand as the bullet had struck. I was up and down those last few steps in a leap to land on the body lying there on the floor, breath being expelled from both our bodies as I landed, but at least I was still holding my gun.

'You bastard,' I managed to get out as I hit the face with the gun butt and in doing so, knocked his head to one side and I could then see who it was. 'Lewis?' I think it was the fact that he was more out of breath than I was and unable to react as quick as me.

'Why Lewis, why?' I cried as I rammed the muzzle of my gun up under his chin, still panting and trying to ignore the pain in my arm.

'Because the promotions are about to be announced,' he gasped, 'as Jackson's about to retire.'

'So?'

'You're to get the Middle East desk. My desk! The one I've worked years for. Mine!'

'Oh you bloody fool,' I hissed at him. 'I've just sent in my resignation to Jackson. It would have been yours without this.'

'Too bloody late now, for both of us,' he said, and I heard the loud click.

When you hear that click, you know you've only got seconds to live, for the sound of the pin being pulled letting the lever go of a grenade means its live. It takes longer to tell you in this one sentence of what went through my brain in that fraction of a second from hearing that noise. There was no point trying to find if he still held the grenade in his hand or let it loose. I wouldn't have the time to find it or get it from his hand if he still held onto it.

I smashed the gun butt into his face as I reared up from him and leapt for the settee and used it as a spring board to bounce and increase my forward momentum as I threw myself at the windows of the cottage. I tried to raise my left arm to protect my face but couldn't lift it and therefore hit the glass and woodwork with that before my shoulder did. I felt the glass cutting me as I smashed through in a shower of glass and wood splinters to land heavily and roll away from the parlour as the grenade detonated. The settee as well as Lewis took most of the blast but there was still a lot of force in the explosion. I was still rolling, naked in the garden and got hit by bricks, glass and timber as well as a cloud of dust as the room exploded in one deafening roar.

I lay choking in the billowing dust, feeling pain everywhere as my ears rang to the noise for several moments before getting up, with some difficulty to my knees. Even though I was only about ten foot away from the cottage, I couldn't see much from the dust that had yet to settle, but I could see a flicker of flame that was cutting through it. I could then just hear the screaming of Mary coming from upstairs that made me get upright and stagger back through this large hole in the parlour wall.

I was oblivious to the cuts I was getting to my bare feet as I clambered over the rubble to see that fire had taken a hold of the room and that half of the staircase that led upstairs was missing.

'Mary!' I screamed out, still hearing her, to my ears, faint cries from the bedroom. 'Mary? Can you hear me?'

'Michael? Is that really you, Michael?' I heard faintly.

'Yes, Mary O'Sullivan, it is,' I shouted up from what had been the bottom of the stairs. 'Get out of there quickly. The place is on fire!' I think Lewis must have brought a can of fuel with him to burn the place after he had killed me, for one end of the parlour was now well and truly alight. There was no sign of him, but all the walls that I could see in that firelight were covered in blood and gore. Then Mary appeared at the top of the stairs, a sheet round her as she stared wild eyed down at me.

'What happened?'

'Tell you later because we've got to get you down from there fast.' I moved over to where the shattered staircase ended in a six foot drop to the littered floor of the parlour. 'Come down as far as you can, carefully. Then jump and I'll catch you.'

'I can't move. I'm frightened!' she cried.

'For Christ's sake, Mary O'Sullivan! Come down and jump or you'll burn to death!' I cried out, starting to feel the heat as the fire grew, growing at an alarming rate. 'I love you, Mary O'Sullivan,' I screamed up at her. 'I don't want to lose you like this!'

There were tears in my eyes as well as in my voice and I think it was this that made her begin to move. She stupidly held the sheet round her with one hand so only had the other to touch the wall, giving her no support whatsoever. She was only on the third step down when what was left of the staircase began to give way. In retrospect it was funny to see her release the sheet to try and find something to hold onto as I then saw her lovely naked body illuminated by the fire light come falling down at me. Her body slammed into mine as I tried to catch her, my left arm refusing to move and one handed was no good as I fell back from the force and felt my body again take more punishment to my back from rubble and splinters and my front from her weight. She cried out as I did as she felt her body being cut by the glass that was sticking out of me and driving it deeper into my flesh. It still didn't stop her from kissing me as she cried both in relief and pain before getting up and helping me rise to my feet.

As she grabbed the bed sheet, I helped her with my good arm across the debris of the parlour to the hole in the wall as the fire was now starting to be really felt on our backs. The garden was just as bad for glass, wood and bricks as we made our way out of the garden and into the field of Meadows Farm where we finally sat down away from the burning cottage. Oblivious to her own nakedness, Mary started to pull pieces of glass from my body that was being reflected from the flames that now had control of the lower half of the cottage.

Wincing as each piece was being extracted from my flesh, I could see that the neighbours on either side of Nick's place were out in their gardens and had already started to spray water from garden hoses onto the thatch of their own cottages. This was in case any of the now rising burning wisps of straw came over to their property and I think that someone by now would have called the fire services.

It was only now, sitting on the grass as I suffered the torment of Mary pulling bits of glass out of my body, did I give thought to what had happened over the last five minutes or so. Lewis, my field officer, my friend, or so I thought. Jealous because he had found out that I was going to be given a desk in the office that he had coveted for years. If only he had said something! He could have had it as I didn't want that position. I would rather have done the training side than be tied like that and not have the freedom that I had been having in the past. When Mary lifted my left arm did I come back from retrospection, crying out as she moved it to pull yet some more glass from me.

'What the hell went on in there?' she was saying as I looked up into her dirt and smoke smudged face, streaked with clean paths of her tears. 'I was pushed out of bed onto the floor to be quiet. Then gunshots and an almighty bloody explosion. The place on fire and you covered in blood and all this glass. When's it all going to end, Michael O'Farrell?'

I grinned with pleasure at that last piece she said in spite of the pain she was causing to my external body. It had provoked a bloody good feeling inside me to hear her say what she did say, causing an erection to start.

'Mary O'Sullivan! Did I hear you right? Would you mind changing your name from O'Sullivan to O'Farrell?'

'No, you stupid man,' she said as she kissed me, both of us wincing as our cut lips met.

'Then I, naked Farrell out here in the grass, ask you, naked Mary O'Sullivan, if you would marry me, for better or worse.'

'What could be worse than this?' she said as she kissed me and said yes.

'Then make yourself decent and go and find if they're sending out an ambulance as well as that fire engine I can now hear in the distance.'

She grinned and tore a piece off the sheet to cover my middle section and the erection that she could clearly see, before wrapping what was left of this dirty and bloodied sheet about herself, covering those delectable breasts to move down to one of the other cottages to ask my question.

I watched as she went down, shrouded in that sheet and as she disappeared, watched the roof of Nick's cottage collapse and get consumed in the fire that the oncoming fire engine had no chance of saving. All it could do when it did arrive was to spray the other cottages first and then damp down the burning remains. In the dying firelight, I could see Mary, now with a coat round her, directing some men up to when I still lay and loved her in spite of the mess she looked then.

Two burly firemen carried me down to meet an arriving ambulance and helped get me inside on a stretcher as I now found it difficult to walk due to the glass still in my feet. Mary came with me to the hospital as she too needed treatment for her feet, though it was my arm that was causing me the most pain.

The bullet from Lewis's gun had chipped the bone but not broken it, but had severed a couple of muscles which were then sewn back together in their fashion on the operating table. They also removed ninety nine per cent of the glass and splinters from my body as well as seeing to Mary's feet.

They kept me in hospital for three days and I got a telegram from Jackson while in there asking me to see him immediately. I got Mary to send one back with the short words of being unable to comply due to incapacity. Lo and behold, he turned up himself the next day.

'Well, you survived and sorted it all out then,' were his first words to me as I lie there on the bed.

'Thanks. I'm feeling much better now,' I replied sarcastically.

'I can see that otherwise I would have asked,' answering me in the same tone. 'Do you mind leaving us alone for a moment?' he asked, turning to Mary.

'She stays!' I said most emphatically, taking hold of her hand. 'You've received my letter I presume?' He nodded but looked displeased that I was keeping Mary in the room I was being held in.

'Well it's not accepted! The promotions are about to be announced and you figure in them,' he said somewhat pompously.

'Like me getting the Middle East desk,' I said sourly.

'Yes,' he said somewhat surprised. 'How did....Lewis?'

'Yes, and as you are retiring, I might suggest you retire Joan at the same time. It could only have been her to leak the information to Lewis if you didn't tell him first.'

'Point taken and you may be right. Well, are you coming back to take it over?'

'Excuse me for one minute,' I said to him. 'Mary? When, or rather after you get your doctorate in psychology, where had you planned to practice?'

'Well, I haven't given it much thought yet but I suppose it would have to be London, why?'

'So,' ignoring her question, 'if I could teach you Arabic?'

'Hold on there a minute,' Jackson interrupted. 'Are you suggesting what I am thinking?' he asked.

'Yes, but you won't be there because you'll have retired,' I said sweetly. 'You'd be getting two for the price of one. How would you like to be working under me, Mary?'

'I love it when you speak dirty,' she said with a wicked grin that was directed at Jackson as well as to me.

'This is going too far,' Jackson spluttered.

'Both or neither,' I told him, and he spluttered some more but finally agreed as long as she signed the Official Secrets Act.

This was done. She signed not only that, but the register in the church that we got married in six months later. Not long after that, she came with me to a birthday party and stood in the background with the other adults as I had the children all sitting in a semi circle round me in a darkened room that was lit by one solitary candle.

'It was a dark and stormy night,' I began, 'and it was in the thrashing down rain that I came face to face with the headless horseman.'

'Excuse me, Mr Farrell, but how can you come face to face with a headless man?' came a voice out of the gloom.

'Ah, our young Miss from last year. Well, it was like this.....'

The End

Here is a sample from another story you may enjoy:

Gay Romance Erotica

Coming Together

Amy Redek

I always thought that I would fall in love sometime in the future but never in a hundred years would I have believed that it would be with be with another man. When at school with the boys, dog-eared books would be passed around showing women, at the beginning, being fully clothed and as you turned the pages, the clothing became scantier with every page until you finally got to those that showed them naked.

I didn't realise at the time why they didn't turn me on. I would see the girls in our class and couldn't stand the way that they would look at you and start giggling and couldn't relate them to the pictures I had seen in the books that had been passed round. They were all flat chested and wore hideous clothing which is maybe what turned me off of them.

It was the same in college. At least there, the girls wore decent looking clothes and filled out the blouse or T shirt that they wore. But again, there wasn't anything special about them that would draw my attention to them. I would even have them smile at me on occasions especially when I was a member of our swimming team.

I must admit that I looked strong and healthy, having loved swimming for years prior to joining the team and so had strong looking arms and chest as well as solid thighs. I never dreamed at the time that what they looked at most was what was hidden inside my swimming costume when I left the pool to return to the changing room.

I would look into one of the mirrors above a wash basin to see what they could see. My face was straight as was my nose. My hair was a cross between being light brown and blonde and my eyebrows were straight and the eye lashes a normal size. My eyes were of a light to dark blue and my smile was okay and it showed that my teeth were good and white. I would even flex my muscles to see that didn't have any effect on me, never giving a thought that they were probably looking much lower down my body at the time.

When we had a college ball, I would spend most of my time with the other boys and wouldn't accept any offers to dance with the girls that asked me to dance with them. I would then often get strange looks from the other guys but nothing was said as to what they were thinking, but I know better now. It was later in reflection that I came to realise that they assumed with me not talking about or going out with any of the girls that I was gay. This thought never came into my mind.

I did well enough at the college to be among the top five and to get an offer to be sent off to a university to expand my knowledge on ancient history, me having come out top of the class on the subject. I had always loved reading books of the period which helped in my achievement at the college.

So off to our local university I went and it was there that I fell in love. It was there that I met Alex who was studying the same as me, and it began with us comparing notes as to what we did or didn't know in the sphere of the ancients. I was following Alexander while he was learning more of Hannibal. Maybe it was because of Alexander being gay that attracted me to his life and connections to others of the same ilk. It was never known if Hannibal was gay or not, but with the men of both armies being away from home for months and years at a time, many of them had sex together without there being any women in their armies to satisfy their need for sex.

It didn't take long for both of us to find out we were both semi historians and so would spend time together to discuss what we each were aiming at. We had different rooms allocated to us but with a little persuasion, Alex got his roommate to swap over with me. So in the evenings after lights out in bed, we could still continue with the pros and cons of each other's subject.

We had our likes and dislikes and compromised to both enjoy being with each other. The major difference between us was that I was a swimmer, which he wasn't, and he was a ski fan, which led us on to want to teach each other of the two differences in our sporting activities. There wasn't any snow near the university but it had a swimming pool, so it was me first to show and teach him how to swim.

It was a twenty-five-metre long pool and had a small trough round on the inside to take the overflow of water that was being constantly pumped out into the pool to keep it fresh. This was ideal for him, when we were in the pool at the shallow end for him to grip this trough and stretch himself out for me to hold him so that he could follow my instructions on how to use his legs. It was also to increase the muscles there, which was much needed in swimming.

It was a good job that my waist was below the water level, for with my left hand under his chest to keep his front end up, my right hand was up under his groin so that he could thrash his legs. The problem for me was that with my right hand where it was, I could feel his penis that was inside his costume and for some inexplicable reason, my own penis would become enlarged to then be a rampant cock.

If you enjoyed this sample then look for **Coming Together.**

Here is a preview of another book you may also enjoy:

THE
AWAKENING

The Daemon Romance Chronicles, Book 1

BOOK OF SHADOWS

Darla Dunbar

THE LAST customer of the day was slowly leaving. Phoebe reached down to pet her dog, Ace, and moved to close up shop. Since graduating high school, she had worked in fairs across the country as a fortune teller, saving money. She did not know why, but when she touched somebody's hand, she could read their thoughts. Although she could not divine their future, she could make educated guesses that were enough to bring customers back. After saving enough money, she had finally opened up her own shop.

Removing the scarf from around her hair, Phoebe let her red curls cascade along her shoulders. Ace sniffed at some of his dog food while she reached over to grab her purse. Before she could close up, a knock at the door surprised her. In front of the door, she saw one of the most gorgeous men she had ever laid eyes on. Curious, she opened the door and let him in.

"Hello! How can I help you, Mr...?" She paused and waited for him to respond.

"My name is Apollo Mikos. Pleasure to meet you, Phoebe Williams." The blonde-haired man reached for her hand and shook it. Instantly, a vision arose before her eyes of Apollo and her rolling around in bed sheets. Waves crashed outside the window—a storm was brewing. As the vision of Apollo entered her body forcefully, Phoebe pulled her hand back. The vision went away, but it left a slight blush on Phoebe's cheeks. Reading the minds of other people was occasionally embarrassing and often felt like a major invasion of privacy. Still, she found herself wishing that she could have held his hand a little longer to see where these thoughts took her.

Motioning toward the table and chairs reserved for clients, she asked if he wanted to sit down. Apollo just shook his head.

"I need your help with something, but not like that." He shrugged his shoulders. Tall and well-built, Apollo had blue eyes and chiseled features. He wore a dark black suit that made all of his muscles ripple beneath the fabric.

Confused, Phoebe looked over at him. "What do you mean?"

Sighing, Apollo looked into her eyes. "You will probably want to sit down for this." Still uncertain, Phoebe sat down and waited for him to speak again.

Gazing out the window, Apollo framed his thoughts. "I know your mother, Rhea. I also know what you really are and I need your help."

Phoebe was aghast. "What do you mean? I don't have a mother. I grew up in foster care after my mother left me there when I was two."

Apollo shook his head. "Before you were born, your mother was raped. They never found who did it and Rhea lived in constant fear. Soon, she discovered that she was pregnant with twin girls. She planned on naming one Cassandra and the other Phoebe. Due to stress, genetics, or just bad luck, Cassandra was stillborn. For a long time, your mother managed to hold it together and take care of you. From what I've heard, the trauma of the rape and having to see a reminder of it every day was too much. She gave you up. The added stress of losing a daughter caused her mental state to break, and she checked into a mental institution."

Leaning back in the chair, Phoebe tried to take it all in. This stranger was telling her things about her life that she didn't even know.

"How do you know all this? And if it's true, where is my birth mother?"

"I know you must have a lot of questions, but for the moment, I need your help." From the back of the room, Ace growled slightly. Phoebe didn't notice the growling, but Apollo shot a wary eye at Ace.

"What could I possibly do? How do I know that you are telling the truth?"

Apollo shrugged. "I could take you to your mother and she could tell you. Then, we can move on to the step where you help me."

The desire to meet this mystery woman who had given birth to her so long ago was too much. Phoebe nodded her assent and grabbed her jacket. Leaving Ace at the fortune teller's hut, she got into the car with Apollo. As he opened her door, her hand brushed against his arm. Reading his mind again, she saw an image of herself thrown back onto the table and Apollo drawing a knife down her body. It didn't look threatening in the vision. Instead, it looked like some type of foreplay.

If you enjoyed this other sample, then look for **The Awakening by Darla Dunbar.**

From the Author

Check my page on Amazon and my blog for Updates and interesting info.

Author Central – http://www.amazon.com/Amy-Redek/e/B00A48NQ72
Author Blog – http://amy-redek.awesomeauthors.org/

If you enjoyed any of my books then please share the love and click like on my books in Amazon.

If you write me a review and send me an email I will send you a free book, or many.
(Just know that these emails are filtered by my publisher.)

Good news is always welcome.

One Last Thing, For Kindle Readers...

When you turn the page, Kindle will give you the opportunity to rate this book and share your thoughts on Facebook and Twitter. If you enjoyed my writings, would you please take a few seconds to let your friends know about it? Because... when they enjoy they will be grateful to you and so will I.

Thank You!

Amy Redek
amy_redek@awesomeauthors.org

About the Author

George Eliot was a famous writer, though at the time, only male authors were recognised. It was in fact the pen name of Mary Ann Evans, a female.

When I started writing, I thought that if a woman could use a male name, why, with me being male, why couldn't I use the name of a female? Though to be different, I made my writer's name from an anagram of my real name.

I wasn't the brightest spark in my school days and it was only while being in the Merchant Navy did I self-educate myself. That being mostly literature, classical music and artists, like Tolstoy, Chopin and Rembrandt. After leaving the navy, I had several jobs, finishing up by being a working boss using my own maxim that 'Management is the art of delegation.'

It's when I became self-employed that I began to write, though sadly, not many of my books can be published because of certain laws that forbid certain aspects of life. This never fazed me for I was really writing just to please myself having a wide range of the human psych.

Having written ninety stories, my only aim now is to reach one hundred. I give thanks to the publishers for at least putting some of my efforts out for others to enjoy as much as I did in the writing of them.

www.ingramcontent.com/pod-product-compliance
Lightning Source LLC
Chambersburg PA
CBHW071341130626
46556CB00004B/1976

* 9 7 8 1 6 2 7 6 1 9 7 4 5 *